D1456321

DOSVIDANIYA
A Story of Love in Revolution

Valentina Ratschenko

DORRANCE & COMPANY

Philadelphia

AUTHOR'S NOTE

The story and characters in this book are a product of the author's imagination.

Dedication: to love

My love had come to me in silence,
In silence did it depart.
Yet the impact that it left upon me
Affected the world in which I live—
Never to be the same again.
                              by Valentina Ratschenko

In memory of my father

My love she speaks like silence
Without ideals or violence
She doesn't have to say she's faithful
Yet she's true like ice like fire.
— Bob Dylan

ACKNOWLEDGMENT

For their spontaneous aid and encouragement, my deepest thanks to my husband Guenther Mueller and my children Jens, Desiree, Joy, Edward.

PREFACE

As soon as I, Alexander Arkadeowitch, finish writing this narrative, I will put a bullet through my head. What follows may look like a novel, but, in reality, it is a great Russian suicide note. I find myself trapped in a vacuum of time. It is a bubble from which there is no escape. I sense the world around me, but the sights and sounds no longer penetrate my being.

I live only in the past and the past is nowhere. I write now only for myself. I want to relive once more the time when I was truly alive. I want to relive once more the experience of Natasha. The narrative that follows is based on her diaries, which I have only recently read.

I

The unfamiliar countryside lay quiet as Natasha watched it from the window of her compartment. The long tired train moved very slowly. Natasha wondered if she would ever reach her destination. Nevertheless, she was determined to enjoy the long-awaited train ride. The train carried her over the mountains and through the valleys where once, long ago, Tartars slaughtered her people and burned their villages. It all took place centuries ago, but the stories and tales lingered on.

Invaders no longer roamed. Now, there was only the soft tall grass that covered the gentle hills. The hills stretched for miles on end, and then slowly faded away, as they blended into the surrounding meadows. The only sound that disturbed the soundless valley now was the gentle twittering of the many thousand birds.

The locomotive went huffing and puffing along, shattering the sleepy quiet of the countryside. Like a weary snake, it twisted through towns, between hills, along cool rippling streams, and then into dark forests, only to emerge once more in order to confront the brilliant sunshine that illuminated the river Don. The train hurtled on, bringing Natasha ever closer to her destination.

It was June, the month in which nature awakens in all her green splendor. As the train rushed by, Natasha could see the aspen trees tremble like a young girl on her first date. June looked forward to summer the way a young girl looks forward to her first love. The recent shower had left everything more lovely and fragrant. The fresh breeze carried the freshness of the early morning; it promised a prosperous harvest.

Natasha was a girl who did not miss a thing, especially when it came to nature. She was fascinated by things that most people ignore completely—such things as the dew upon the petals of a water lily, or the raindrops that lay heavy upon the fragile new leaves. How everything danced in the warmth of the sun! The butterflies seemed to be weightless as they fluttered in the early hours of the day.

The young girl tried to catch the remote sounds that floated in upon the breeze. She loved every part of nature—especially the blue clear streams of her homeland, the gentle silver birch trees, and the wind that moved it all. But there were moments when tears would fill her eyes and her heart would become heavy as she watched the wonders around her. She could not tell whether they were tears of happiness, or tears of sadness for all that had passed away in order to make room for the rest. Or, perhaps, the tears were for the expectation of the unknown days that were to follow. The days to come would bring changes—in her own life, in the whole country. She could not understand it then. But she felt it. And it felt sad. Sad and painful.

She must have fallen asleep for quite a while. The sun was much higher now, and was brightly shining upon the scattered fields and rooftops. It was hot and uncomfortable. Natasha opened a window and allowed the wind to blow through the long thick hair which hung loosely about her shoulders. The ends of her hair were sticking to the base of her neck, and this was making her uncomfortable. "Ah, this feels better," she said, as she opened the top buttons of the soft pink blouse that her father had brought back from his last business trip to Paris.

The cool breeze soon refreshed her. She was still bothered, however, by the prospect of the long journey alone in her compartment. The compartment was small, and this made it all the worse. She was a little angry at her father for insisting upon a private compartment. He knew how much she disliked being alone. But, father had told her that if she did not like the idea, she could stay home. She thought it was unfair, but she had to agree. She was an obedient daughter and so there was nothing she could have done. The more she thought about it, the more perturbed she became. "What possibly could happen to me on a train?" she asked herself. For the first time in her life she regretted the fact that her father was so rich and influential. If she had come from a poor family, she would not have to suffer being alone. "Why does he still treat me like a child?" she thought. "I am a big girl now and capable of taking care of myself."

Unconsciously, she straightened up, as if to reassure herself once again that she really was a big girl. She smiled as she took a long look at herself in her small hand mirror. The mirror was set in gold with her name engraved on the back. "I am a big girl," she told herself with a voice of authority. "I am seventeen. I am a woman."

But there were things about her that made her doubt whether she really was a woman. She still had small breasts, and this worried her. She wondered if they would ever grow. She thought of the times she had cried upon her mother's large bosom. This made her sadder still.

"Why do you worry your pretty little head, my child, about things that are so unimportant. Give them a chance to grow. You are still so very young," Maria Ivanovna, Natasha's mother, had said trying to comfort her only daughter. Natasha was all that she had left. Her two boys had died in battle just over a year ago, and she was still stricken with grief.

Maria Ivanovna was right. Natasha had nothing to worry about. For Natasha had so much more in her favor than most girls her age. She was a well-educated, soft-spoken young lady. Her slender figure and medium height complemented her manners and spirit. But the thing that her mother most appreciated about her daughter was her disinterest in an early marriage. As long ago as her mother could remember, Natasha had determined to devote herself to becoming a fine artist. Everything else was secondary.

As Natasha reminisced, the train moved on.

"Oh well," Natasha thought, "only a few more hours and I will be in Soshi." That thought made her blood rush through her veins. She felt her cheeks get warmer as she thought of Grisha. She remembered that she had loved him once. But she was only a child then. She wondered what she would feel for him now. "I know that it is going to be a wonderful summer," she said to herself. And, once again, she drifted deeper into her thoughts and tried to imagine how everything would be.

She watched the little village they were passing. People were

3

busy attending to their everyday chores. Children waved to the passengers on the train as it went by. The train left a big cloud of smoke behind, that lingered for a while and then slowly disappeared like the long awaited train itself.

Villages like this one were worlds unto themselves. The people never knew nor cared to know of any other place. They were born here, produced a new crop of children here, and died here. That was all there was to it. They never saw another part of the beautiful country that surrounded them. They were too poor and too uneducated to care to learn what lay beyond the horizon. They were content just having enough bread to feed their children and themselves.

The almost cloudless sky was a special shade of blue. Here and there hung perfect white clouds. They hung motionless, like large mirrors reflecting the things below. Natasha wished that everything could be as peaceful and quiet as the splendor in front of her. But, inside her heart, she knew that was impossible. For, behind those trees and inside those houses, there was hunger, pain, despair, and tears. The village was beautiful to a rich passerby. But it was a beauty ready to explode.

Natasha's thoughts were interrupted by a knock on the door. She could not believe her eyes. One of her lifelong friends was standing at the door and she had no idea why.

"Petja! Petja Sokolow!" she said with excitement as he entered her compartment.

"Good morning, Natasha. It is nice to see you again," he said shyly.

"And you don't know how ecstatic I am at finding you here. Where are you traveling?"

"Nowhere. I work on the train."

"So that's the reason we haven't seen you for some time."

"Can I get you anything, Natasha?"

"Thank you, but I'm fine. Company is the only thing I long for."

He remained a moment longer, brushing his bushy reddish hair out of his face, which was almost transparently pale. His oversized ears glowed bright red as the sun shone through them.

"How about a cup of tea?" he said smiling.

"That would be nice. But where will you get tea on this train?" Natasha asked.

"I have my ways," he said with male boastfulness.

He came back almost immediately, bringing with him a cup of tea which he took out of his own meager rations. As she drank the tea the two of them talked of old times. They talked about Natasha's family, and the games that they used to play as children. Both of them avoided any discussion of Petja's family, especially Petja's father, who was a drunken and brutal man. Natasha shook her head from side to side, as she remembered the welts that she used to see on Petja's back when they went swimming together.

Deep within himself, Petja had a love of Natasha that went far beyond gratitude, and he had a lot to be grateful for. Natasha had taught him how to read and also to appreciate the finer things in life, like music and poetry.

Natasha remembered that Petja wanted to be a teacher when he grew up. But this dream was destined to go unfulfilled. His father had been killed in a drunken brawl, and now the sole support for his mother and the nine children rested on Petja's narrow shoulders. There would be no time for school.

After Natasha had finished her tea, Petja took the cup and, with deep regret, went back to his menial job of porter.

After lunch, the train passed another small village, which consisted of about a dozen mud huts whose worn and sunken roofs looked as if they would blow away in a strong wind. The small village was divided by one dusty street and was surrounded by wheat fields. The village lay quiet, too quiet in fact, for that time of the day. Natasha was wondering where everyone was. Not even children were seen, only some dogs and chickens moved in the hot midday sun.

The train pulled out around a bend and came into a clearing. There, Natasha saw a sad procession, marching slowly toward the cemetery, which lay in the distance. "I wonder who could have died? A mother? A father? Maybe a small child?" But, whoever it had been, she found it especially nice of everyone to have taken time out from their busy day in order to accompany that departed individual to his last resting place. The soul that shared their sorrows and their joys would remain in their hearts forever.

Funerals depressed her, especially since her two older brothers were killed somewhere on the battlefields of Russia. She shook her head as she always did when she wanted to rid herself of a bad thought. She tried to forget the past and, instead, visualize the happy days that she was going to spend with her dear friend Katya.

Natasha had not seen much of her childhood friend since Katya had married and moved away to the Black Sea. But Katya's new life had not kept the two friends apart. They had their precious letters. Natasha was overjoyed when she finally received an invitation from Katya, to come and spend the summer with her. "Finally, I will be able to see Katya's beautiful home," she told her parents. Her parents had expressed much anxiety about the proposed trip. They felt that it was too dangerous for her to make such a long trip in troublesome times. Time and again they tried to convince her of the wisdom of their judgment. Yet Natasha's parents could not remain insensitive to her entreaties for long. Reminded of Katya's mysterious illness, they finally succumbed to Natasha's pleas. They granted her permission to visit Katya. That was three days ago, and now Natasha was almost there. Her heart jumped with joy at the thought.

She thought about Katya and her mysterious illness. Natasha hoped that it was not serious. Once again, she had to shake her head, in order not to think about sad things. To rid her mind of the unwelcome thoughts, she concentrated on the days when they were children and the good times the two of them had had together.

The train was traveling in flat country now. Tall and mighty trees rushed past. The train went by fields where peasants bent low and worked with sweat running down their faces and backs. The gentle warm wind blew past the new soft grass, making it shimmer like silver stripes of tinsel. Natasha counted the church towers as she came closer to her destination.

Katya was three years older than Natasha, but the difference in age never really mattered to them. They meshed together like two finely tooled gears. Their friendship matured with age. They learned from each other and shared joys, disappointments, and secrets. They also shared a deep passion for flowers, poetry, and the other small things which are so important to young girls.

Katya always wore a big smile. She was always cheerful; almost nothing could dim her spirits. Being gifted with a strong soprano voice, she would sing like a nightingale from the moment she awoke in the morning until she said her prayers at night. She was liked by everyone. And, as soon as she was old enough, there were more boys after her than she really cared for.

Katya had beautiful blond hair, blue eyes, and was very well built. Natasha envied her friend's womanly figure and her silken blond hair. In contrast, Natasha's hair was black like the night, and her eyes were green. Natasha was a little taller and slimmer than Katya. But there was one thing that Katya did not possess — patience and the ability to be serious for a moment. And that's where Natasha far surpassed Katya. For where Katya was short on patience, Natasha was over-blessed with it. Her mother would scold her for spending many sleepless nights working on one of her projects and forgetting everything else. "Child, why are you so serious?" Natasha's mother would ask her. But she would not wait for an answer. It amused her to see her husband's serious expression on her young daughter's face.

Natasha and Katya enjoyed every free moment they had together — playing in the sand as children, or lying in the tall green grass that hid them from the rest of the world. They felt free to dream of the beautiful things of life that awaited them. Sad things never entered their minds. As far as they were concerned, they would live happily ever after. Yes, and it looked as if the two of them would never be able to live apart from each other.

As Natasha looked back on the summer that had separated them, a shiver ran through her whole body. She blushed with embarrassment at the memory of her childlike behavior, when Katya had told her about the man she had fallen in love with.

7

She could still remember the foolish words she had shouted when Katya tried to tell her about the young stranger she had met the day before.

"You don't even know that man! How can you love someone that you don't even know? And besides, what are your parents going to say? You know they won't stand for it."

"Natasha, it is true that I just met him yesterday," Katya replied. "But I know how I feel about him. It is a feeling I have never felt before. Natasha, I know it sounds strange, but I feel as if I have known him all my life. Oh, Natasha, it is a wonderful feeling to be in love!"

"But why? Why did you have to fall in love with him? What about the other men that are interested in you?"

"But I am not interested in them. Can't you understand that?"

"Then, what about Boris? You know how he feels about you. How are you going to tell him about the stranger?"

"Natasha, you are being childish, and you know it. You know how I feel about Boris. I have never promised him anything, and he knows it."

"But what about the understanding between your two families?"

"I don't care what his father is going to think or say. As far as mamma and papa are concerned, they will understand and be very happy when they get to know Grisha. I am sure of it."

"Oh, and you call him 'Grisha' already! Shame on you, Katya Fredrowna!"

"Natasha, you are still a child. Wait until you fall in love. You will also talk differently."

This was the first time that Katya had called her a child, and it hurt. What Katya had said proved to be correct. Her parents were surprised at first, but easily adjusted to their prospective son-in-law when they found he was a bright lad from a good wealthy family. Katya was married that same summer; she had a traditional wedding with all the trimmings. And, after a few days of celebration, Katya left her father's house and moved to the Black Sea to start a new chapter in her life.

At first, Natasha was greatly upset. However, after Katya's

letters started coming with regularity, Natasha reconciled herself to the situation, and came to share vicariously in Katya's happiness. Natasha, once again, became absorbed in her own studies, and before she realized it, three years had passed.

The train continued on.

II

The long gray train entered the city of Soshi. Soshi is a typical harbor city; it is busy and filthy and smells of fish. But none of this dimmed Natasha's excitement. Soon she would be with Katya and Grisha, and this was all that mattered. As the train slowed down, Natasha collected her belongings. She combed and arranged her hair, and draped a blue velvet cape behind her back. After she had said good-bye to Petja, who helped her get her things off the train, she began trying to find Katya in the crowd. Her eyes scanned the many faces, but she could not see Katya anywhere. Strangers stared at her as they scurried past. She decided to stay in one spot and let Katya find her.

After a few moments, she found herself alone on the platform. Ten minutes passed very slowly. As she waited alone, a feeling of disappointment developed inside her. She figured that Katya was probably just a little delayed, and she picked up her bags. Natasha had decided to wait outside the station.

Natasha did not wait long before she heard her name being called. At first, she didn't know if she should turn around. The voice that she heard was not that of a woman, but a deep, harsh, male voice. Turning around, she saw a man approaching her. He walked with a slight limp. All she saw was his warm smile. His hair was neatly combed to one side. The man was tastefully dressed, reflecting wealth and position. He was Grisha Grillow, Katya's husband. Natasha's heart beat quicker. She hoped he could not hear it.

"Sdrastwujte, Natasha Borisovna," Grisha said, as he extended his hand to her in greeting. "I am terribly sorry for being late," he apologized. Grisha noticed that Natasha's eyes were not on him. They were still searching for Katya. "You are looking for Katya? I am sorry, but she did not come along."

"Oh," she said, with obvious disappointment.

"Katya wanted to come, but I insisted that she stay in bed. It is a very long journey to the station, and I thought the ride

10

would be too much of a strain for her. I hoped you would understand."

"Of course, I understand. But I was under the impression that Katya was feeling better."

"She has been much better, especially since she received the news that you had agreed to spend the summer with us. Do you regret that I came instead of Katya?"

Grisha still held Natasha's hands, and he gazed at her intently. He was amazed at how much she had grown in the last three years. She was now almost as tall as he was. And her slender body had taken on pounds where it mattered. Yes, she had blossomed into a beautiful young lady, whose every fiber breathed life. A faint smile warmed her face, while her green eyes sparkled with all the expectation and trustfulness of youth. It was a sparkle that had been missing from his wife, ever since her illness.

Natasha's tapered fingers felt warm, as she tried to wiggle them out of his hand. But he held them a moment longer.

"I am not disappointed in seeing you. It is just that I was expecting Katya. That's all." She blushed as Grisha complimented her on having grown into a lovely lady. She still could not receive compliments without blushing.

"I am surprised, Natasha. I expected to find the same child who hated me three years ago, when I stole her best friend." Grisha spoke easily with the self-assurance of a true gentleman.

"Did it show that much?"

"Certainly. But I hope your feelings for me have changed in the interim?"

"You know that they have. Does that please you, Gospodin Grillow?"

"It pleases me very much, Natasha Borisovna."

They exchanged smiles, delighted to know that they understood one another. Taking her by her arm, Grisha led Natasha to his carriage. After she was seated, he put her belongings in the back and then took his place beside her.

As they drove through town, Natasha looked slightly uncomfortable. She was not accustomed to seeing so many people at once.

"Looking at you, I get the feeling that you don't care for big towns," Grisha said. "I can understand that. You see, I feel the same way. Big towns are exciting only at night. That's what I think."

"I think so, too," Natasha replied, not really understanding what was meant.

"But you have nothing to worry about. Where we live, the nearest neighbor is an hour away. I hope that you will not find it boring."

"I won't. How did you know what I was thinking?"

"It is your lovely face. It is very expressive. It reveals all the secrets of your soul."

"Really now, Gospodin Grillow!" Natasha said indignantly.

Natasha looked at him now for the first time. She was glad that he looked just like she remembered him. He was just as charming as ever and just as polite. Grisha did have a few silver gray hairs that were not there before; but, if anything, this served to improve his looks. He seemed so much older the first time she had met him. Then again, she was so much younger then.

But there was one change that she noticed that was not good. This was a certain sadness that played in his dark eyes, even when he smiled. His eyes seemed even more enigmatic and dark. They seemed to hold a certain mystery in them — a mystery that she could not yet fathom.

"You must be exhausted from that long train ride," he said, reaching for the reins.

"I'm fine, thank you. But, I will be glad when I get out of these clothes. I feel like I have had them on for the last week."

"I know what you mean." Taking the reins between his slender fingers, he gave a shout, "OK, Storm, on your way!" The beautiful horse took off and soon the bustle of the town was left far behind.

Soon they were galloping along a country road that led them through fields of corn and potatoes. Storm followed the path without having to be directed, for the intelligent animal knew this road well. He had traveled it often with his mistress, Katya. But not recently. It had been months since Storm had heard Katya yell, "Faster, faster," with her long blond hair blowing in the wind as the carriage sped along. Yes, those were the good old days that the beautiful animal now missed.

Katya waited anxiously for the carriage to return with her beloved husband and dear friend. She closed the window in order to keep the hot noon sun out of her room and stretched herself out on the red sofa that stood in the middle of the room. Freshly picked red roses perfumed the dark room, leaving a sweet and heavy odor. This, however, made her even more tired. She knew now that Grisha was right to insist that she wait at home. She knew how lucky she was to have Grisha. He had been a pillar of strength throughout her long illness. His presence had almost made her fate bearable.

But, there wasn't much that Katya had been able to give him in return. For the last few months, she hadn't even been a wife to him. They had moved into separate bedrooms at the doctor's insistence. And yet, he never once complained when he had to say good-night and go to his lonely room down the hall.

He didn't have to complain! She knew how hard it was for him. Sometimes she would watch him when he didn't think she was looking. Grisha's gentle face would crack with pity, and tears would sometimes streak it. He tried very hard not to break down in front of her. He knew what it would do to Katya. And she loved him even more for his concern.

He was the one that never gave up hope, and he was the one that told her not to lose it either. She wished that there was something she could do for him in return. There was nothing in this world that she wouldn't have done for Grisha. With his name on her lips, she fell asleep.

Natasha and Grisha rode together in silence now. They searched in their own hearts for answers to questions that were not yet asked. Natasha admired the beautiful carriage. She had never seen one that was quite as magnificent. The outside of the carriage had a white trim embossed with a gold design. The interior was bright red, with red leather cushions. The reins were decorated with bright shining bronze buttons that glistened like stars. Natasha later learned that the carriage and stallion were the wedding present that Grisha had given Katya. Consequently, they had special meaning for Katya, and she

13

cherished them as symbols of her husband's love.

At a fork in the road, they turned south. They passed acres of orchards, which exuded an intoxicating aroma of ripening apples. With the sun in her face, Natasha had some difficulty seeing straight ahead. Yet, from the scenery she had already noticed, she became slightly jealous of her best friend. Katya lived among so much beauty, and had a husband like Grisha as well.

"I hope Katya realizes what a lucky girl she is," said Natasha.

Grisha did not answer; he did not even hear the question. When he finally spoke, his voice was heavy and deep. He spoke slowly and methodically, as if to make sure Natasha understood every word.

"Natasha, I would like you to know how much I appreciate your coming to spend the summer with Katya and myself. You do not know what this means to us. I thank you from the bottom of my heart." He did not look at her as he spoke, but kept his eyes on the road ahead. He was a man who did not show his emotions easily; he preferred to keep them all to himself, as if they were some kind of treasure.

"But, I am the one who should thank you and Katya. If it weren't for the two of you, I would never have had an opportunity to see this magnificent country. I thank you, Gospodin Grillow."

Grisha looked at her for a long moment, and after giving her a warm smile, he turned his gaze back to the road. He was afraid that she might read something in his eyes. He did not want her to taste the grief and pain that had dulled his existence. Nevertheless, despite his efforts, Natasha could not help but sense that something was wrong.

"I know it is none of my business, but is there anything wrong? Does my presence bother you?" she finally asked, unable to restrain herself any longer.

"Now, whatever gave you that idea?" He pretended not to know what she was talking about.

"Oh, it's just that you have been so very quiet." And then after a moment of thought, she added, "Or, are you always like this?"

14

"I have been quiet, haven't I? I am sorry for that, and I do promise to be better company from now on."

As they approached the blue sea, the breeze became stronger. It seemed to penetrate Natasha's very being. Her eyes remained fixed on the wide, blue sea — the sea that in the years to come would always fascinate her. Natasha did not quite believe that she was really here. She felt at one with nature and knew that, as long as she felt this way, she could do no wrong. For her, nature was a teacher — a teacher that taught her strength, gentleness, and beauty.

"See that white house over there? That's our home," said Grisha.

It was impossible to miss the white mansion, which the setting sun adorned with a golden halo. The two story manor house stood raised above the surrounding orchards. Tall trees hid the peasants' huts from view. From Katya's letters, Natasha felt that she knew the house intimately, even before seeing it. The long road wound around in gentle curves, as it approached the house. On both sides of the road, there were green lawns and well-tended gardens. It was even more beautiful than Natasha had imagined! To one side stood an old windmill which was no longer in use. Its aged sails and crumbling foundation seemed as old as Russia itself. The whole place seemed a visual embodiment of the Russian folk tales that Natasha loved to hear when she was young.

As they pulled up in front of the house, a tall brown-haired servant came out to greet them. Natasha later learned that old Stopa was more than just an employee. He had been with the family for years, and was now considered an integral part of it.

"Sdrastwujte," Stopa exclaimed, as he took hold of the reins that Grisha handed to him. He stood admiring the long-awaited visitor. It was Stopa who had picked up Natasha's letters in town and brought them to the estate. He never tired of hearing Katya's stories of the childhood days she had spent with her best friend. He noticed how his mistress's face would brighten and her spirits lift, as she recounted to him the happy days of their youth together.

"Natasha, I want you to meet Stopa Tobenow, the man who

makes this place work," Grisha said by way of introduction.

"Pleased to meet you, Gospodin Tobenow."

"And I am very pleased to meet you," Stopa said. "I feel as if I have known you for a long time now." He shook her hand warmly. "Please do not hesitate to ask for anything."

"Thank you, Gospodin Tobenow." Natasha liked Stopa right from the start. She liked his smile and his humble ways of saying things — the way he held his pipe, and the way his hair would fall into his eyes, making him appear like a young schoolboy. He made her feel right at home. Natasha felt an immediate friendship for Stopa.

Grisha helped Natasha out of the carriage. Meanwhile, Stopa led the stallion away to the stables. Natasha followed Grisha up the wide stairs that led into the spacious and elegantly furnished house. The rooms were large, without seeming desolate. The colors were bright and warm. Comfort and love were felt as soon as you entered.

The first room she entered was a huge reception hall. The room was lit by three large chandeliers that hung from the second story ceiling. There were many majestic archways leading off the main room. Two towered over large bay windows; the rest were doorways that led into other parts of the house. The floor was covered with tiles of Italian marble. The decor of the room matched the bright blues and reds of the tiles.

Through one of the doorways, a wall of glass could be seen. Fascinated by it all, Natasha had forgotten completely about Katya. Without even asking permission, Natasha went into the other room to have a better look at the view. A flaming sun was setting into the horizon of the sea. It was a mist-free day, and miles of white-capped water stretched into the distance.

"It is just as lovely as Katya has written to me," she said, turning around to face Grisha.

Grisha stood by the door and watched Natasha. "Katya spends a lot of her time in front of this window, Grisha said. "It is one of her favorite places, especially when she is writing to you."

"And I can see why. But where is Katya?" Natasha asked with great concern.

"She must be in her room. Why don't we go up and surprise her. She must have fallen asleep. She is very weak, you know, and tires very easily." Grisha took Natasha by her arm and led her up the stairs.

As they climbed the stairs, great tapestries could be seen hanging on the walls. Between the woven treasures were portraits of two generations of Grillows. When they entered Katya's room, they found her sleeping peacefully. Natasha wondered aloud, "Perhaps, it would be better to let her sleep now. We have the whole summer ahead of us to spend together."

"I don't think that would be a good idea," Grisha said. "She is going to feel bad enough as it is, when she finds out that she had been asleep when her guest arrived." He walked over to his sleeping wife and kissed her gently on her thin lips that were tightly closed. "Wake up, my love. We are back."

At the sound of Grisha's voice, Katya opened her eyes. Her sleepy glance fell upon Natasha, who was standing behind Grisha. Natasha was smiling, but her eyes were filled with tears, as she fell into the open arms of her lifelong friend. After a few warm kisses and many tears, Katya was the one who spoke first. "My dear Natasha, I can't believe that you are really here. You've come from so far away. Will you ever forgive me for sleeping through your arrival?"

"But Katya, there is nothing to forgive. I am glad that you had a good rest. I have so much to tell you that we will probably be up half the night." Natasha knew that Katya would be interested in a complete account of the latest news from back home. "Katya, you are looking well, extremely well, in fact. Are you sure that you weren't just fooling when you wrote that you were not well?"

"No, Natasha, I didn't fool you. But, as you can see for yourself, I am fine now—at least now that you are here, my dear friend."

Grisha stood back, out of the way, forgotten for a moment. He listened in silence. He smiled, trying not to show that his heart was breaking in two.

Katya released Natasha and took a step back in order to better see her friend. "Now, let me look at you," she made

Natasha turn around. "You look simply beautiful! How much you have grown. Isn't she lovely, Grisha?"

At first, he just stood there without saying a word. He pretended that he was seeing her for the first time. His lips formed into a self-conscious smile. "Yes, my dear, she is a very pretty young woman." Natasha was blushing now, at being made the center of attention. Grisha, seeing that he was embarrassing her, excused himself by saying, "I think that I better leave you two alone. You must have things to talk about that you don't want me to hear. And, besides, I have my own work to do."

It was after Grisha had gone, and the two of them had settled down a bit, that Natasha noticed a trace of sadness on Katya's face. "Why so sad Katya?"

"I am not really sad, Natasha. I have tears of joy at seeing you again." Katya, however, was not telling the full truth. Inside she knew that she was dying.

"I hope so," Natasha said, "because I am so glad to see you again."

"There is so much that I want you to tell me," Katya said. "I don't know where to begin. But wait, I am being inconsiderate. You must be exhausted. You should go now and freshen up. We have all summer to talk. The trip must have been very tiring."

"It wasn't all that bad," Natasha said. "And, besides, I had some company, if only for a short while. Petja Sokolow, you do remember him?"

"You mean the one with the big ears that had his eyes on you ever since I can remember?"

"Oh, come on, Katya. Don't start that again."

"Well, you know it's the truth. How is he?"

"He's fine," answered Natasha, wishing that she never had mentioned his name.

"I haven't seen him for over three years. Has he changed much?"

"Not really. But, he has grown awfully tall."

"Is he still so funny-looking?" Katya asked.

"Not everyone thought he was funny-looking. It was just you who used to make fun of him, Katya Grillow. And, besides, his ears are not really that big. And you know it."

18

"Natasha, I am just teasing you. You know that. But, you were always fond of him. Maybe there is something between you two?" Katya said, with a glimmer in her eyes. Katya's teasing no longer bothered Natasha, as it once did. Now it even amused her.

"What was he doing on the train with you? Did you bring him along for company?" Katya continued.

"He works as a porter on the train," responded Natasha.

"That's good. I bet that he is glad to be out of that house. But, Natasha, you must rest up a bit before dinner. Come with me; I will show you to your room." But as Katya rose, her head began to spin, and she fell back to the couch. The fainting spell soon passed, but she still felt a bit weak and shaky. She lay on the couch, looking up with her big blue eyes at Natasha, who was so conerned that she was almost ready to faint herself.

"Katya, what is wrong? Can I do something?"

"No, Natasha. It is nothing. Just a little fainting spell. It was my fault for getting up so fast. I was told not to do that, but I keep on forgetting."

"Katya, should I get someone to help you?" Natasha asked, feeling helpless in the situation.

"For goodness sakes, no. I will be fine in a minute. It was just a little too much excitement. Natasha, please hand me that green bottle over there."

After Katya had taken the medicine, Natasha placed the pillow under Katya's head and inquired if there were anything she could do to make her more comfortable. It was strange to see Katya so sickly. Katya was always the healthiest person Natasha knew. This was the first time that she saw her weak and fragile. It filled her heart with panic.

"Natasha, I wanted to show you to your room, but I think it would be better if I continue to lie down for a while. I am really sorry to have scared you so."

"Don't worry about that, Katya," Natasha said and tried to smile a little.

"You'll be able to find the room easily enough," Katya explained. "It is the fourth door to your right."

"Don't concern yourself about my room. I will stay with you until you feel better. Then I will go and find the room myself."

"I must insist that you go now. I will be fine, really!" Katya said, hoping that she would be able to collect herself after her friend left.

"Are you sure that it will be all right to leave you alone?" Natasha asked unsurely.

"Of course. Go now, quickly. Please." Katya did not want Natasha to see the tears that were ready to roll down her cheeks, tears of self-pity. Before Natasha left the room, Katya added, "You don't have to tell anyone about this spell of mine, you know. It really isn't anything to get concerned about."

Natasha was walking to her room, when Grisha came up the stairs.

"Come with me," Grisha said, "I will show you to your room."

She followed him into a large airy room. The room was furnished with fine furniture. Chairs were upholstered with blue velvet, and, on the floor, there was a Persian rug. The long slim windows were covered with soft white lace curtains. The window was open, letting in the fresh air of the sea.

The familiar smell of freshly picked flowers filled the room. On the table next to the window, there stood a large bouquet made up of many different shades of flowers in a careful arrangement emphasizing the long wavy brown petals of the lady's slipper, which stood alert and startled, high above the rest. Natasha ran her fingers along the familiar lines of the leaves, and inhaled the sweetness of their scent.

"Katya picked them this very morning," Grisha said. "She thought that they would make you feel more at home."

"Oh, they do. The whole room is just perfect for me."

Grisha's eyes could not hide his pleasure, and he turned to leave.

"Gospodin Grillow, I want you to know that you and Katya are very special people. I thank you for inviting me to spend time here with you. This is surely going to be one of the happiest summers of my life."

"The pleasure is all ours, Natasha. Now, I'd better leave you alone so you can do whatever women do. Is there anything I can get you before I leave?"

"No, thank you. No . . . wait . . . there is one thing. Would you check on Katya? She was feeling a little faint. But please, don't tell her I told you about it."

"My poor Katya. I guess she had a little too much excitement for one day. By the way," Grisha remarked, "we have our dinner at seven. That doesn't give you much time. Marusia will be with you in a moment to help you dress."

Natasha stood at the window. The sun's reflection shimmered in brilliant colors, while the water rushed toward the sandy beach. It splashed against the mighty rocks, which held the rich soil responsible for the splendor and abundance of nature's yield. Below her window, there was a spacious flower garden. Elegant white statues stood in just the right places to harmonize with the landscaping. The water from the fountain spurted high into the air and then fell back, refreshing the lily bed.

The setting of the sun began to throw shadows upon the objects below. The huts of the peasants looked gray now. Only the rooftops were still lit up by the last rays of the sun. There was a knock at the door.

"Come in," Natasha said. A plump and elderly woman entered. "You must be Marusia."

"Yes, I am." Marusia put some water in a large basin and closed the windows.

"Katya has missed you so much," Marusia said. "Your presence here makes her very happy. God bless you, my child."

"I do hope that is true," Natasha replied, "Katya's happiness is quite important to me."

"Now, you must hurry," Marusia warned. "It is almost seven o'clock, and dinner is served on time in this house."

As soon as the woman had closed the door behind her, Natasha swiftly undressed, washed as well as she could in the short time left and donned a red gown that was slightly wrinkled from being packed.

When Natasha descended the stairs, she found Katya, Grisha, and Stopa in the dining room. Grisha rose and helped Natasha to her seat.

"Katya," Natasha said, "it was very thoughtful of you to remember the flowers. They are so lovely, and you know they are my favorite."

Tonight, dinner was a special occasion. Instead of the usual serious faces and talk of strikes and farming, there was laughter and light conversation. The two girls reminisced about home and all their old friends. After dinner, tea was served in the sitting room, which was also a library.

Katya began to play the piano, while the others listened. Natasha's eyes wandered around the room. She was fascinated by the beamed ceiling and the oak paneled walls. One entire wall was covered with books. Bound in fine leather, these volumes were written in six different languages, and spanned the arts, sciences, history, and philosophy. From Katya's letters, Natasha had learned that Grisha had read every one of the books. Only now did she realize the full enormity of the accomplishment.

In the huge parlor, there were two groupings of furniture, one by the window and the other close to the library. The heavy chairs and sofa were covered in sumptuous brown leather. Near the couch was a round table, displaying many precious family pictures. In the right corner of the room hung an icon of Our Lady of Vladimir, which was one of Natasha's favorite saints. The golden frame was illuminated by a candle which was kept burning at all times.

After Katya completed the rhapsody, she and Natasha gossiped about old times. Grisha and Stopa were discussing some estate business on the other side of the room. Usually Grisha did not care much for the silly laughter of women, but now he loved the sound of it. The whole family were enjoying themselves so much, they hardly noticed the hours that passed.

As the evening wore on, Grisha reminded Katya that it was long past her bedtime. Reluctantly, she went to her room, insisting all the while that she wasn't really tired. Ascending the stairway, Katya asked Natasha to remain in the parlor to keep Grisha company.

"I think that I'd better get some rest myself," Natasha said. "It has been a tiring day for me. I don't think that I would be very good company tonight."

Back in her room, Natasha undressed. Before retiring, she opened the window that Marusia had closed. The gentle sea breeze again filled the room. Exhausted from her trip, Natasha fell asleep immediately.

Natasha arose late the next day. She slept through the morning and stirred only at lunch time. She had needed that rest. Now she felt refreshed and full of energy.

The summer days that followed were the most beautiful that Natasha could remember. She became enchanted with the cool ocean breeze, and it became a vital part of her. She never missed the setting of the sun, especially on the days it formed a big orange ball that slowly rolled into the dark sea. At night, she would watch the moon and stars from her balcony. But, most of all, she treasured every moment that she spent with Katya.

Natasha's presence seemed to bring Katya back to health. The two women went on long rides together. It was the first time that Katya had been on a horse in months. They took walks into the fields that were covered with wild flowers, and lay on the ground reading poetry to each other. It looked as if Katya had forgotten about her illness. Unfortunately, she was soon again to remember.

As the weeks passed, Natasha began to notice that they had to restrict their activities more and more, because Katya wasn't able to keep up the pace. She would tire easily, and her midday rests became longer. Natasha found herself alone more often, but she did not mind it at first. She was always able to keep busy, even if she were just walking or going for a swim. Natasha was happy and content.

But, as Katya's health continued to deteriorate, Natasha became increasingly worried. Whenever she would ask Katya what was really the matter, she would never get a direct answer. Natasha tried not to think about it; but, whenever she would see the lost, frightened look in her friend's eyes, haunting thoughts would return and leave her no peace. Soon they had to completely eliminate their walks. Katya was forced to spend most of her time in her room. At night, she asked to have her dinner served in her room also. And so, the three of them would eat in the bedroom with her.

One night, after saying good-night to Katya, Natasha went downstairs to talk to Grisha. As she entered the sitting room, Grisha remained standing with his back to the door, looking out into the dark night. Seeing her reflection in the glass, he said, "Come in, Natasha."

"Are you sure I am not intruding?" she asked, when he did not even bother to turn around.

"Of course you're not intruding," he said, turning now to face her. The empty look on his gentle face soon revealed that something weighed heavy on his soul, and Natasha could guess what it was. Now that she saw him, she was hesitant to disturb him with any questions.

Even from a distance, Natasha had learned a lot about Grisha. She called him Grisha now. She learned about the things he liked and about the things he didn't like. She could tell when he was happy, and when there was turmoil behind his dark eyes. Even so, they had rarely been alone as they were now.

Every time she saw him come into the room, her heart would stir. The very sound of his voice was something magical that turned the everyday world into something special. The most awkward times, however, were when their eyes would meet, or when she would feel the brush of his hand upon hers. This would send chills down her spine. Now, she understood how Katya must have felt, when she first fell in love with Grisha. She thrilled in the understanding, but the thrill was tinged with guilt. So Natasha hid her feelings and tried to stay out of his way. She wondered if the others could see how she felt.

"Grisha, there is something that I would like to ask you," she finally said.

"Please sit down," he said, pointing to an oversized red chair.

Sitting in the chair, she appeared even more slender than she actually was. She waited for him to sit down before she continued, but he remained standing, looking down at her with his hands behind his back. He already knew what she was going to ask him. He had noticed the worried look in her eyes, as Katya's illness became worse.

"Grisha, I have been worried about Katya's health. She is

getting worse instead of better. Is there something seriously wrong with her, something that I don't know about?"

He began to pace back and forth in front of her. He rubbed his hands, trying to stall for time. He knew how much the truth would hurt her and make her life seem empty and meaningless. It was just a few months ago that he had to come to cope with it himself. At that time, he thought that he would not be able to go on. He prayed that the doctors were wrong. He prayed for a miracle. For a while, after Natasha came, he thought the miracle had happened. But no, now it was worse than ever. All the symptoms that he had been told to look for were there to see. Now, it was just a matter of time, and he knew it.

"Grisha, you can tell me. Please. I have to know," she insisted. "I know that there is something terribly wrong. I've sensed it ever since I came, despite your trying to hide it."

"Natasha, you are right. There is something terribly wrong with Katya. She is a very sick girl."

The silence that followed lasted only a few seconds, but it seemed like an eternity. The only thing that disturbed the solemn seconds was the old clock that kept on ticking. He went over and sat down across from her. Looking at her and trying to find the right words, he did not know how to tell her the terrible news.

"Natasha, Katya is never going to get well, never," he finally said.

Not quite understanding his words, she asked, "What do you mean, 'never'?"

"Exactly what I said. She is never going to get well, Natasha, and she doesn't have much time left."

All at once, everything around her seemed unreal. The voice she was hearing seemed like an echo that came to her from a far distance. She thought that she was going to cry, but, surprisingly, no tears came. She sat there, numbed, with her hands flat on her knees, and stared at Grisha. She did not see him, though. All she could see was Katya's dear face slowly fading away.

Then she heard a voice asking what really was wrong with Katya. She did not even realize that it was her own voice.

"She has some kind of blood disease," Grisha said. "It is

called leukemia — acute. There is nothing anyone can do for her." He told her about all the doctors that he had taken Katya to see — the best specialists in the country, the best that money could buy. No one could help her. "If only it could have been me instead," he said.

Then, finally, Natasha asked the question she hated to ask. "Does she know that she is going to die?"

"Yes, that's the reason she asked you to come," Grisha said morosely. "You know, that was her only wish when she found out that she was going to die. The only thing that she wanted was to spend her last days with you at her side."

Grisha rose and went to the window. He looked out, but he could not see far into the dark night. He listened to the violent splashing of the water. "Do you know that there were moments when I was actually jealous of you," Grisha finally said. "Can you believe that? I am ashamed of myself for being so selfish; but, I would have hoped that I would have been the only person she would have wanted to see at a time like this." He could not go on for he was now crying like a child. He looked so helpless and alone.

Natasha got up as if hypnotized and put her slender arms around him. She held him close as he continued to cry. She knew what he was going through. She ran her fingers through his dark full hair. It was like a mother comforting an injured child. For a little while, all that Natasha could think of was Grisha. It was only later that she remembered Katya and the fact that her death was imminent.

That night Natasha hardly slept. By the time she finally fell asleep, it was dawn. As she closed her eyes, she could hear the first sounds of morning. Another day had already started — a day full of life and promise. But not for Katya.

The days that followed were hard for Natasha. She tried not to show the pain that she felt. But it was so hard to conceal that she even began to play with the idea of going home. But, whenever she suggested it, Grisha would always talk her out of it. She wondered sometimes whether she was staying because of Katya, or because of Grisha. Now, Natasha seemed to be two different people. When she was with Katya, she tried to be happy and inspiring. But when she was alone, she was always sad and gloomy.

One delightful Sunday afternoon during tea, Katya kept staring at Natasha, who looked particularly lovely in her blue silk dress. But Katya also saw in Natasha an extremely sad girl, whose cup was shaking as she picked it up and brought it to her lips.

"Natasha, do you feel like talking?" she finally asked. "I know something has been bothering you. I have been watching you. What is it that makes you so sad?"

"It is really nothing," Natasha said defensively.

"I think I can make a very good guess," countered Katya.

"What do you mean?" Natasha asked innocently.

"You have found out about my illness, haven't you?"

Natasha hesitated at first. She did not want to answer, but she knew that she had to. At last, she said, "Yes, I have."

"I was hoping that you would leave before finding out. But I guess that was impossible. It must be awfully hard on you my dear Natasha. How did you find out?"

"Grisha told me," she answered, not knowing if she had said the right thing.

"I asked him not to do that. But maybe it is better this way," Katya said.

"It wasn't his fault," Natasha replied. "I made him tell me. Katya, from the moment that I came into this house — in fact, even before that, when Grisha picked me up at the station — I felt that there was something wrong. And when I saw you getting weaker each day, I knew that I was right." She could not hold back the tears that were filling her eyes. "Well, at least it is in the open, now. In a way, I am glad that you will not have to pretend any longer."

The hands with which Katya held Natasha were cold. Soon they began to tremble, as tears ran down Katya's pale cheeks also. Her cheeks had once been round and full of color. Now they were emaciated.

"We should not give up all hope," Natasha said. "The

doctors will find a solution. I know they will. You must have faith. Try not to think about it."

Natasha got up and went over to the open window and inhaled the fresh air, as if that would provide her with new strength. She needed the strength in order to withstand Katya's sad face, a face which had lost all of its sparkle of youth.

Katya came over to her, and together they watched the pounding surf, which was so lovely and dear to them both. Katya loved this house and her dear husband who shared it with her. How it hurt to see him suffer and worry. She had wanted to make life easier for him, but all she gave him now were sleepless nights and gray hair. He was one of the reasons that she had asked Natasha to come. She hoped that Natasha would bring a little joy into Grisha's life. She even thought that it would be a good idea for Natasha to marry Grisha after she died. She knew that Natasha would make him a good wife, and bring him happiness and a son. That was all that mattered to Katya. But, Katya was disappointed, when she saw that Natasha was ignoring Grisha and forcing him to spend the long evening hours alone.

Natasha watched a yellow butterfly circle above. Katya interrupted the silence that separated the two friends. "You know that there are times when I think that I am going to lose my mind," Katya said. "Especially when I see the lovely things that are out there. I am going to miss every little part of this place. And when I think of my Grisha, oh, how my heart hurts knowing that I won't be with him much longer. And even our friendship will soon end."

"You may think it strange," Natasha said, "but I believe that our friendship existed long before this lifetime and will continue long afterwards. We will remain forever as close as we are now. I don't think that a friendship like ours can develop in one lifetime."

"I think that you may be right, Natasha. You are so wise."

"No, I'm not wise, but I have strong beliefs about some things that are important to me."

"Our friendship has been a very special one, hasn't it?" Katya said wistfully.

"It is very special," replied Natasha. Tears of pity could still be seen in Natasha's eyes as she continued. "How I wish that I could make things easier for you."

"At times like this, one can only turn to God," Katya said. "I thank Him for every moment that He has given me. I thank Him for giving me you as a friend. There is nothing more worthwhile in this world than true friendship. It is something rare and precious." Katya lowered herself slowly into a nearby chair and continued. "And then, there is my Grisha. How lucky I am to have known such a love. I am, indeed, a very lucky woman, to have had all these things even for a short while.

"So, listen to me now and remember what I am going to tell you. You must live a full life, and don't be afraid to live it the way you feel you want to. It is your life, and yours alone. Once your time comes to go, nobody can come and say, 'let me go in your place.' So, please, promise me. Let something good come out of all this. Now, come, and let me see that smile of yours."

The big red ball of fire was slowly disappearing behind the trees, while the evening breeze moved quietly over the foliage. Everything seemed peaceful and content. The sweet summer air lingered on into the night, making it a melancholy lonely evening.

While walking that evening, Natasha thought about the things that Katya had told her. Her words brought to mind her own father's words. "Child, if people would only live each day as if that were their last, they would live a full and rewarding life. They would be the better for it." Yes, that was her father's philosophy, and, now for the first time, it made sense to her. Never before did she really understand it. She had never been aware of death as she was now. When her brothers had died, they had died for a cause; but Katya's coming death was different. Her death would be a senseless one. Natasha felt like she better understood the meaning of life. One must live each day at a time, and accept what lay on the path ahead with grace and thanks.

The days that Natasha and Katya spent together now were devoted mostly to reading or doing some kind of handwork, which Katya still enjoyed. Whenever Katya was sleeping, Natasha would write letters back home, or swim, or simply sit on the rocks and watch the water as it splashed against them. Sometimes, she would even get wet from the spray. Or, she would take off her shoes and walk along the shore, dodging the waves as they would come rushing by. She needed these moments alone in order to gain strength.

She saw Katya's eyes wherever she went. It was an empty stare that looked beyond what was there. Katya's strength was fading faster now, like a tired sun that was determined to set. Natasha tried to snap her out of it, by holding her tight, or reading to her from a favorite book. Katya would always be thankful for Natasha's efforts. But there were also moments when Natasha, herself, would weaken. At times like this, she was incapable of saying anything encouraging. She would run to her room and cry, knowing full well that crying could change nothing.

One afternoon, as Natasha was leaving Katya's room, Katya suggested, "Natasha, how would you like to paint a portrait of me?"

"That sounds like a wonderful idea, but, you know, I am not a good artist yet. I haven't done many portraits."

"You are very good. Don't berate yourself like that. Remember years ago, you promised to do a painting of me some day. Now is your chance."

"But Katya, I have no paints, or anything that I need."

"That is no excuse. You can go into town and get all that you need."

Natasha thought for a while and realized that Katya was right. Painting Katya's portrait might make things easier for both of them and brighten Katya's days. "Well, OK," Natasha said, "but, I can't promise that it will be a masterpiece. I'll do my best."

Katya's face lit up with excitement. Her body tensed as if already posing for the portrait. "Good then," she said. "We will start as soon as possible. How about tomorrow?"

"It's fine with me," Natasha replied.

Grisha had to go to town on business the next day and promised to take Natasha along. Because of the rebellion that was brewing, it would have been unsafe for her to go alone. It was still early in the morning when they left the house. Natasha wanted to be back early, before Katya would really miss her. Now that Natasha had decided to resume painting, she could not wait to start. She missed her easel and paint brushes more than she had realized.

Natasha had always found painting to be very soothing and relaxing. On canvas, she was able to capture all the vividness of life. It was the only way that she could express herself honestly. Since coming to her friends' house, she had made several sketches of her favorite places, and hoped later to reproduce them on canvas.

When Grisha and Natasha set out, the plains were still covered by a low fog that had come in suddenly the night before. Soon, however, a hot sun burnt it away, leaving a clear view in all directions. But, Stopa had predicted rain, and now it looked as if he would be right. Dark clouds were slowly moving in from the north, covering more and more of the blue summer sky.

After a little polite conversation, the two rode in silence for some time, each absorbed in his own thoughts. Natasha was thinking about the man at her side, who still remained somewhat of a mystery to her. His quiet reserved way made him appear always to be withdrawn and guarded, which made it difficult to get close to him. And that was what she wished to do more than anything else. She wanted to explore the depths of his soul, and she knew no way to penetrate his world. But she did know one thing, and that was that she loved him. She had no idea how he felt about her. Rarely had more than a dozen words passed between them. Nonetheless, she knew that she would do anything for this man. But there was still Katya. These thoughts disturbed Natasha. She shook her head from side to side.

Natasha tried to compare Grisha to Dr. Arkadeowitch, the man who expected to marry her. There was nothing enigmatic about him. He was an easygoing, open person. Many women back home were attracted to him and would have been happy to be his wife. In the presence of Alexander, she felt mature and self-assured. With Grisha, to the contrary. She felt nervous, and sometimes acted childishly. Natasha wondered

31

how she could love a man that made her feel so uncomfortable. She prayed that no one would find out that she had fallen in love with a man who was already taken. She wondered why she didn't feel about Alexander the way she felt about Grisha. If only she could, everything would be fine.

After riding a while, the quietness became embarrassing. Natasha was the first to speak.

"Grisha," she asked, "what do you think about all the new uprisings among the peasants and factory workers? Do you think that it will come to anything?"

His face darkened even more as he answered. "I really think so. The people want a change desperately, and a change is desperately needed. I only fear that their valid grievances will be exploited by the wrong kind of people."

"Yes, that would be a disaster," she agreed. Natasha didn't think very seriously about politics, however. Politics does not usually concern young girls who have more important things to think about.

Natasha stared at Grisha and he felt her gaze upon him. He turned and looked at her for a long time. He started to say something, changed his mind, and said something else instead.

"Natasha, I want to thank you once again for helping Katya. You have been an angel."

"Oh, I am not, Gospodin, I mean Grisha. You don't have to thank me. My reward is just knowing that I am able to help in some small way. I only wish that I could take more of the burden off you."

"But you do," Grisha said. "Katya needs somebody to stay with her all the time. Somebody who is a friend. You have made her very happy." He put his warm hand over hers to show his appreciation, and she saw the faint trace of a smile on his lips. She did not move her hand away, as she always did before. Now, it felt good and right, and she enjoyed the warmth of his hand.

"Natasha, have I done anything to hurt you?" Grisha said suddenly a little while later.

At first she was shocked and couldn't figure out what he meant. Finally, she asked, "What do you mean?"

"Well, you have been ignoring me ever since you arrived."

"That's strange," Natasha said. "I had the same feeling about you. I thought you were avoiding me."

"I am truly sorry if I have given you that impression. But I guess it must be hard on you at times to put up with my moods. You can understand that Katya's illness is very difficult for me. You know what she means to me. I don't know what I will do without her. But I should not take it out on you. Let us start all over again, and be friends. Is that a deal?"

"It's a deal!" she assured him.

"I'm glad at least that's settled," he said. He gave a shout, as he pulled on the reins, "Come on, Storm. A little faster, we don't have all day to get to town."

Up ahead, Natasha could see the town. When she was last here, she had been happy and full of expectation. Now, a month later, everything was different, different and more confused. Though it was still early, smoke could already be seen rising out of the chimneys. The voices of children could be heard singing as they played. The streets were crowded with workers walking to the factories. It was nice, for a change, to see so many people. In the excitement, Natasha was able to forget about Katya for a short time. Even Grisha was different. He wore a warm smile and was kept busy returning greetings from passersby. It seemed as if he knew everyone in town. It also seemed as if he had left the big house behind him, and, with it, all the pain that his home life meant.

The stores were still closed, and they would have to wait half an hour for them to open. In the meantime, Grisha and Natasha decided to have breakfast in a small restaurant that Grisha knew by the waterfront. It was a cozy place that was run by a husband and wife, both of whom looked as if they enjoyed their own cooking; between them, they probably weighed five hundred pounds.

As soon as they walked in, the old man greeted Grisha in a familiar way.

"It's good to see you again, Gospodin Grillow." The owner's happiness was not feigned. Besides being a friend, Grisha was quite a generous tipper.

"Good morning, Sergei Sergeowitch. And how are you this lovely day?"

"Very good, very good," the old man said.

"Sergei, I would like you to meet Natasha Vasilowna Borisovna, Katya's best friend." Grisha turned to Natasha. "Natasha, Sergeowitch is the best cook in town."

"It is a pleasure to meet you," Natasha said, looking forward to the meal.

"Is the stove already lit?" Grisha asked. "Natasha and I are starved from the ride into town. What do you have for breakfast?"

"I will prepare something special for you, something that I make only for very special customers," the old man said, speaking from somewhere behind his thick beard. He showed them to the best table in the restaurant, which also happened to be the only table. The table faced a large window through which it was possible to see the tall-masted cargo ships entering and leaving the harbor.

The old woman brought out a platter covered with salmon, smoked ham, hard-boiled eggs, homemade bread, and several kinds of jams. As Grisha and Natasha ate, they could see the storm clouds roll in. It was going to rain for sure. They ate in a hurry, because they did not want to be caught in the downpour.

"Be careful of the sailors," Grisha said, as he prepared to go about his business. "I will meet you across the street in an hour."

Natasha watched him get into the carriage and drive off. She then walked across the street and into the general store that Katya had told her about. The store had a little of everything, from sewing needles to horseshoes. Before long, Natasha had collected all the equipment she needed, including some personal items, such as stationery and a present for Katya.

While she was waiting for Grisha, Natasha heard a voice behind her. She turned around and saw an old sailor. The sailor had long red whiskers, with only a few rotting teeth showing through them. He kept both hands stuffed in his pockets. He was carefully balancing himself, as if he expected a wave to come at any moment and tilt the sidewalk.

"Hey, little lady, where do you live," the sailor said, speaking in some far-off accent which Natasha could not identify.

"Girlee, I'm speaking to you," the sailor pressed further after Natasha ignored him.

"I do not speak to men to whom I have not been formally introduced," Natasha finally said.

"Why don't you come back to my hotel room for a little drink," the sailor persisted. He moved closer to Natasha, close enough for her to smell the alcohol on his breath.

"Leave me alone," Natasha said. "I want nothing to do with you."

"Ah, come, Galubchick. We'll have fun. My place ain't far."

At this point, the sailor did something that shattered Natasha's delicate nature. He took his right hand out of his pocket and pointed down the street to the cheap hotel where he presumably lived. He pointed, however, with a hand that wasn't there. What was there was a sharp metal hook. At the sight of the hook, Natasha began screaming. She continued to scream long after the sailor ran down the street and disappeared into an alleyway.

Although Grisha returned right on time, it seemed to Natasha as if he had been away for days. She told him what had happened, and he cursed himself for leaving her alone. He helped her into the buggy, and continued to apologize for leaving her alone, until they were several miles out of town.

The sun had completely vanished and the wind began to blow harder. As they rode between the open fields, the wind began to pick up dust and blow it in their faces. The dull roar of thunder interrupted the peaceful silence. Natasha prayed that the angry wind would blow the thunder away. She loved the rain and the wind, but she was terrified of thunder and lightning. As a child, she once saw a cow that had been struck by lightning, and she never forgot what she saw. The further the two got from town, the brighter the lightning became, and the louder the thunder. Natasha's heart beat faster as her fingers clutched her red shawl. If only they could reach home before it got much worse. She did not want Grisha to see what a coward she was when it came to thunder.

As the first raindrops began to fall, Grisha turned off the main road and headed for a nearby barn. By the time they reached the barn, they both were completely soaked. The water ran down Natasha's face, and she felt like a drowned rat. But she had no time to worry about her appearance, for the lightning and thunder crashed over them. The barn was large and easily contained the whole carriage. Natasha found a comfortable spot behind a stack of hay, which kept her from seeing the lightning through the open door. As a further precaution, she closed her eyes.

"I hope it will stop soon," Grisha said, as he unbridled the horse.

When Grisha spoke, Natasha opened her eyes for an instant. It was a mistake. Just at that moment, lightning shattered a large tree that stood just a few feet from the barn door. Natasha screamed so loud that Grisha thought that the lightning had struck her.

"Natasha, are you all right?" he said, half expecting no answer.

At first, she could not say a word. Grisha took her into his arms and held her like a child. He brushed the wet hair away from her face.

"Don't be afraid, my little angel. I will take care of you. Don't be afraid, it's only thunder. It will be over soon."

Natasha found herself relaxing a little. She felt safe in his arms, as safe as being in the arms of her father. She was always sure that as long as she was in her father's arms, nothing could ever happen to her. As Natasha calmed down and was about to let go of Grisha's arm, the lightning struck again. She grabbed him so hard that she was sure that she had done him an injury.

"I am sorry. Have I hurt you?" she asked, after she realized what she had done.

"You didn't hurt me," Grisha reassured her. "Just hold on as long as you want."

"You must think that I am a silly little child," Natasha said blushing.

"I think no such thing. Thunder scares me, also. It scares most people. Even my mother had to hide in the closet when there was a storm."

Natasha looked at him. And, for the first time, she looked deep into his eyes. They were warm eyes, warm and inviting.

Inside her breast, her heart beat out a tune whose melody was unfamiliar to her. It was as if they were seeing each other for the first time. Now, Grisha sensed that his holding her was not right. But, at the same time, he didn't want to let her go. It felt good to hold a warm soft woman. He never thought that he could feel anything for a woman other than Katya. But, here he found himself holding one, and wanting her so much that his whole body ached. Yes, he knew that it was wrong and that he had no right to feel the way he did. They looked at each other for only a few seconds, but to the two of them, it seemed like an eternity. Finally, he let her go gently and he rested. They both felt emotionally drained.

Grisha feared Natasha now, and feared, even more, what might come of their being alone together. He hated himself for not being in control of his emotions. It was almost as if he resented being human.

The storm clouds had moved on. After a while, the sky began to clear, and it looked as if it would be a nice day after all.

"Natasha, I think it's a good time to have our lunch," Grisha said, happy to get back to mundane things.

"But I'm not hungry. All I want is to get back home and dry off."

When you see what I have, you won't be able to control your appetite," Grisha argued. Putting the basket in front of her, he continued, "By the time we finish eating, the rain will have stopped, and we can be on our way."

Natasha soon forgot that, just a short time ago, she had been in a state of panic. She was enjoying the lunch after all. Together, they joked and laughed, until once more the sun was shining.

"Would you mind if we took a little detour," Grisha asked, after they had set out again.

"Of course not. I am always happy to see more of this beautiful country of yours."

"Good, there is something I would like to show you," Grisha said eagerly. He made a right turn at the next narrow road and headed in the direction of the sea. After two miles, they arrived in front of an old cottage.

"This is the place where it all began," Grisha said with a sigh. It sounded like a different Grisha speaking, a Grisha whom Natasha had never heard before. "This is where my father started out forty years ago. This was the first land that he owned. I was born in this little cottage. The mansion was built long afterwards."

They sat in silence for a moment.

"Would you like to see the inside?" Grisha finally asked.

"I'd love to." Natasha dismounted before he could help her down. She watched him open the door with an old iron key, which contrasted with the gold chain on which it was carried.

As they entered the hut, Grisha said, "My father built this house all by himself." Grisha spoke as if in a trance. "I have tried to preserve it exactly as it was then," he said running his slim fingers along the familiar rough walls. Natasha was surprised to find out that Grisha was such a sentimentalist. Until now, she had believed that he was a practical man who lived only in the present.

The small house was clean and orderly. The table was covered by a cloth and flower pots stood on the deep window sills. Grisha led her into a small room that had two cots.

"This was my bed," he said, pointing. "Later, I shared it with my younger brother. And the other bed was my sister's."

"Does anyone live here now?" Natasha asked.

"No."

"But who keeps it so clean?"

"I do. I come here at least once a week."

"Then you must love this place very much."

"Yes," he said. And Natasha could almost picture the memories flashing through his mind. "I feel foolish telling you this," Grisha added.

"I don't think you are a fool," Natasha said quickly.

"You are kind to say so," Grisha responded.

Grisha took Natasha by the arm and showed her into his parents' old bedroom. Natasha noticed that the bed was made and covered with a white linen sheet trimmed with handmade lace. The pillows were fluffed up and, in one corner, there were two icons—one of the Holy Mother and the other of Jesus. Both had scarfs hanging over them, as was customary. Natasha was moved by what she saw, and how tenderly it was preserved. She could almost hear the voices of times past.

"How do you like it?" Grisha asked, after they were outside and ready to leave.

"I think that it is absolutely charming." The place is so much like him, she thought. It was quiet and serene, just like he was. She loved this simple place. And she knew why Grisha loved it. And, because of this, she found herself loving Grisha all the more. "You were happy here, weren't you?"

"Yes, Natasha. I have always dreamed that when I had a son, he would be as happy as I was here." This was the first time that Natasha had heard him mention anything about children.

Grisha locked the door as they left and helped Natasha back into the carriage. "I rarely show this place to people," Grisha said. "I do not think they would understand why I keep it up. Even Katya sometimes teases me about it."

"I really appreciate your showing it to me," Natasha said, flattered. "Back home I have a special place, too, which I would like to show you one day."

"I would love to see it," Grisha said.

Katya was waiting at the front door when the carriage drove up. "Oh, my God," Katya said, "you're both soaked and will catch your death of cold. Go inside immediately and change into something dry." Natasha was pleased to see that Katya looked a little stronger today.

Later that night, after dinner, while they were sitting in the library, Natasha presented Katya with a little surprise. "I hope you like it," Natasha said, excitedly, as she handed Katya a gift-wrapped package.

Katya ripped off the paper, anxious to see what it was. She was overwhelmed by what she saw. "Where did you find it? This is exactly like my old doll."

"Yes, I couldn't believe it myself when I saw it in the store window today. It even has the same dress as your old doll. I knew that I had to get it for you."

"Natasha, you remembered after all these years. Thank you so much," Katya said as she hugged the doll. "Grisha, let me tell you the story behind Natasha and this doll."

"This I have to hear," said Grisha, putting his book aside.

"I think I was only about eleven years old," Katya began, "when my father brought me back a doll like this from Moscow. I never much liked it, but Natasha fell in love with it immediately. She wanted it more than anything in the world. Her father tried to find one like it, but without success. So, Natasha would always demand that I lend it to her. Those were the only times that we ever fought. I refused to give her the doll. Not because I liked it, but because Natasha wanted it so badly. Then I broke down, and, one day, let her keep the doll for a few days. You will never guess what she did."

"She broke it," suggested Grisha.

"No, but, accidentally, she dropped it into the river, and that was the end of the doll, and the end of our fights."

"But I promised you that I would someday give you the same doll back — so now we are even," Natasha said proudly.

"We sure had some good times, didn't we?" Katya said, as she got ready to go to her room. "Good night, Natasha, you don't have to come up with me. I will be fine."

"Good night, Katya. Sleep well. Tomorrow is the big day. We will start on the portrait."

Natasha was glad to have the painting to work on because this kept her busy and out of Grisha's sight. This was just what she wanted, she thought, trying to fool herself. Katya decided to eat lunch upstairs in her room again, and Natasha ate with her. Except for the evening meal, Grisha would eat downstairs with Stopa. Because of this, Natasha and Grisha saw less of each other.

During the day, Grisha was kept busy with the men in the fields. At night, Natasha would go for a walk, so that Grisha could be alone with Katya.

The portrait was coming along fine. She worked hard at it, since she wanted it to be her best picture. It was taking her longer than she had expected, because Katya was able to sit for only short periods.

Katya couldn't help but notice that Natasha was avoiding Grisha; and so, one day she asked Natasha, "Is there something wrong between you and Grisha?"

"Why do you ask? Of course there isn't," Natasha replied defensively.

"Did you fight or something?" Katya persisted.

"Really, Katya, there is nothing wrong."

"Well, you can't deny that you have been avoiding Grisha, can you?"

"It's your imagination," Natasha insisted.

"I really don't think so, because even Grisha noticed it."

"Why, did he say something?" Natasha asked, surprised.

"Yes."

"Well, I think it's ridiculous."

"Natasha," Katya continued, "please be nice to him, if only for my sake. He needs someone. You know how hard it is for him, and I know that, deep in your heart, you have a real fondness for him. It shouldn't be hard for you to be a little more friendly."

Natasha did, in fact, try to make an effort to see more of Grisha, or at least, to make it appear as if she were seeing more of him. The summer was almost over, and soon she would be going home to the man who was waiting so patiently to marry her. She knew that all her anxieties would vanish with her departure; and so, in a way, she looked forward to it. In another way, however, she didn't. And this was to prove to be more important.

One night, as Natasha sat at her desk trying to answer her mother's last letter, she found that she could not concentrate. She tried several times to make a beginning, but ripped up each page after writing only a few lines. I will write tomorrow, she told herself. Tonight, I think I will go for a walk.

The path led down to the water, which seemed exceptionally calm tonight. It was a warm, humid night; the leaves on the trees remained motionless, as if afraid to break the spell of quietness. The last light of the sun was slowly fading away in the distance, while the warm air was perfumed by the smell of wild strawberries which grew along the shore. It was a wonderful night, but not for being alone. It hurt. Natasha was homesick for the first time since her arrival at the Black Sea.

Natasha walked along the water, barefoot, as usual. She

played with the wet sand that caught between her toes. Once in a while, there was a gentle splash of water that washed her feet clean. She smiled and then continued on her way.

By now, the moon was high. It hid, at times, behind a dark cloud, only to show itself for an instant, and then disappear again behind another cloud. The dark rocks looked like gargoyles. But Natasha wasn't scared. She was too lost in her thoughts and feelings to really see them. At times, she thought that she heard something behind the rocks; but, whenever she stopped to listen, all she could hear was the splashing of the waves or the occasional hooting of an owl. Then, she remembered Grisha's warning not to wander far from the house at night. She started to walk back.

When she got within sight of the house, however, she no longer felt any fear. On an impulse, she undressed and ran into the cool dark water. She swam until she was completely exhausted. She did not notice the dark figure standing on the shore until she started to come out. Though the figure was draped in shadows, from its size she knew that it had to be a man. She called out, but the figure neither spoke nor moved.

Natasha decided it would be best to stay in the water until the man moved on. After ten minutes, she found herself getting extremely cold. The figure was still there. She called out again. "Who are you? Go away, please. I beg you."

Again the figure remained still and silent.

Natasha's teeth began to rattle from cold and fear. "Is that you, Grisha?" she yelled, all the while knowing that it could not possibly be Grisha.

As if in answer, there was an awful laugh that filled the silence with horror.

"Stop that. Go away, whoever you are," Natasha said anxiously.

But the man apparently did not even hear her. With his hands at his side, he shook and laughed like an idiot.

By now, Natasha was desperate. Her whole body was numb from cold and fright. She began to swim in the direction of home, hoping he would not see her. She wondered how she was going to get into the house without any clothes on. But, at this point, that didn't matter. All she wanted to do was get away from the monster on shore.

She swam as fast as she could, but the man was able to keep up with her easily by walking along the shore. She stopped and treaded water, realizing that she would never be able to out-swim him.

She was petrified, as she watched the man slowly step into the water. She could see the moonlight reflecting off his long black boots. As the man came closer and closer, Natasha found herself too scared even to move away. Within seconds, he was just a few feet from her. Then, suddenly, he reached out his gigantic arm, and she felt his hand grab the end of her hair. It was while the giant was pulling her naked body into shore that she fainted.

A little while later, as she slowly regained consciousness, she heard what she thought was a familiar voice. It was a few seconds before she was able to identify it with certainty. It was the voice of Grisha.

"Are you all right? Are you all right, Natasha?" Grisha asked imploringly.

Natasha slowly opened her eyes. She saw that she was covered by Grisha's jacket, and that Grisha was huddling over her. And, then, to her right she saw the body of the monster. The monster lay unconscious now in the sand. He lay flat on his back, and the expression on his face betrayed complete surprise at what had layed him low.

What had layed the monster low was Grisha, or more accurately, the handle of the black leather riding crop that Grisha usually carried.

"If I had not come out when I did, it would have been all over for you," Grisha said. "I told you never to go far from the house at night." Now that he was sure that Natasha was really all right, he felt free to scold her.

As they walked into the house, Grisha explained to Natasha that the monster was, in fact, the town idiot, who had been deaf and dumb since birth.

"Why did you come looking for me just then?" Natasha asked.

"I went to your room to ask you something and could not find you there, and so, I decided to go and look for you on the beach," Grisha explained. Together they walked back into the house. Marusia prepared Natasha a warm bath, and after the bath, Natasha got into bed and fell asleep immediately with Grisha's voice still ringing in her ears.

The following evening, Natasha decided to stay close to the house. She sat on the front portico, watched the starry night, and listened to the crickets that filled the evening air with sound. After a while, she felt that she could now finish the letter which she had started the night before. She was about to get up, when she saw Grisha come out of the house.

"May I join you?" he asked, as he sat down beside her. They sat for a while, enjoying the night air. "Would you like to go for a walk?" Grisha asked.

"I don't know if I should," Natasha answered. "I was planning to write some letters that are long overdue."

"We won't stay long," he reassured her. "You will still have plenty of time to write."

Natasha rose to join the man who was already standing and waiting for her. They turned into a narrow path that led through the orchards, which lay checkered in shadows and moonlight. They talked in muted tones as they walked beneath the summer sky. What they said was not important. It was how they said it, and to whom it was said. The air was mingled with the sweet smell of the early fruit, ready to be picked. The moon watched their every move, as if to remind them that they were not alone. But what the moon did not know was that its silvery beams were stirring up a feeling that was so very real and warming to the hearts of those two lonely people, who were trying so desperately to fight it.

They soon reached a clearing where the garden ended and the fields of corn began. The corn stood tall and strong now.

"It was a good year for the corn," Grisha remarked.

Natasha was not really interested in corn, but she politely agreed. She was afraid of being alone with Grisha and wanted to go home. She was afraid of what she might do. The fear made her shiver. She hoped that Grisha did not notice.

Natasha picked up a stem of long grass and played with it in order to keep her hands calm. But, when that did not help, she suggested that they turn back.

"Why?" Grisha asked. "Do you not enjoy my company?"

"Of course I do. It is just that it is getting late, and I am a little cold," Natasha responded, to justify her strange behavior.

"Cold? On a warm night like this?" Grisha asked incredulously. "Are you ill?" He touched her forehead to see if she had any fever. "I would certainly not want to see you get sick now."

Natasha remained silent, as he took her into his arms.

"Maybe this old man can keep you warm," he said innocently.

Natasha let him hold her, but it made her shiver all the worse. He noticed her shivering.

"Why are you so afraid of me?" he asked.

"What makes you think that I am afraid of you?" she said, all the while pushing him away.

"The way you pull away everytime I try to come close to you," he said.

"Don't be silly," Natasha responded. "Why should I be afraid of you?"

"For the same reason that I am afraid," Grisha said solemnly.

"Yes, I know," she admitted, looking away from him. "I am afraid, too. Afraid of myself, and what I might say or do."

He watched her as she stood close to him but free of his embrace. Her face was lit up, while his was in shadow. He forced her to look at him. She looked deep into his eyes.

"It is nice being with you like this," she said, "but it is not right, and you know it."

He came over and took both of her hands into his. He looked into her eyes, which shone like the stars above.

"Those are the sweetest words you have ever said to me," he said thankfully. He brought her fingertips up to his lips and kissed them. "I'm sorry," he said, "it is just that nights like this make me do things that I would not normally do."

"Yes, I know," she said. "It is this melancholy summer night." She was pleased that they had finally found a culprit on whom to blame their transgressions.

As he ran his fingers through Natasha's hair, all of his

troubles vanished for an instant. He forgot all about the political turmoil in his beloved country. He forgot all about his lost youth. But, more important, he forgot about the fact that just two hundred yards away, his wife was dying.

They remained still for a while. And then, Natasha became frightened again, frightened of how far it all might go. She tried to pull away from him, but he held her tight. How wonderful, Natasha thought, to have a man like this hold you. If only there weren't Katya! The thought of Katya, however, made her pull away all the harder.

She broke loose and ran back towards the house. Grisha ran after her. He called her name softly as he ran.

"Natasha!" As he ran, Grisha wondered why he was running after such a very young girl.

Before Natasha could get near the house, Grisha caught up with her. He grabbed her hand and held it. She did not try to pull away, but tried instead to calmly remonstrate with him.

"What we are doing is not right. It is simply not right under the present circumstances. And you know it."

"But, Natasha," he said, pleading. "We haven't done anything wrong. What are you so afraid of?"

"We have no right to be as close as this," she said. "Not with Katya the way she is. We have no right. You are making it very hard on me."

Before either of them knew what was happening, he was kissing her full on the lips. The kiss lasted until their two bodies had fallen back onto the flower bed that lay beneath them. The kiss lasted until their two bodies had become one body. One body amidst a thousand carnations. Sometime later, Grisha kissed Natasha again. Between the two kisses, everything had happened. Everything had happened to transform Natasha from a young girl into a mature woman. The kiss ended suddenly. As soon as he released her, she silently turned around and ran back into the house. She did not look back.

She went up to her bedroom, got undressed and fell asleep, with Grisha's name on her lips and tears in her eyes.

The next morning, Natasha went into Katya's room and tried to act as if nothing had happened. Katya, however, immediately noticed the tear stains under Natasha's eyes.

"Is there something wrong?" Katya asked.

"I'm fine. What do you mean?"

"You have been crying. Your eyes are all swollen," Katya said.

"Yes, you are right," Natasha confessed. "I have been crying. But, not over something important. Everything is all right now."

Katya did not really believe her. "Why were you crying? Tell me the truth. Come sit over here and tell me all about it."

"There is nothing to tell," Natasha said, but then a false reason came into her mind. She sat down, and looked into her friend's white face. She could see how much it had changed. Dark shadows had formed under the eyes, and her hair hung brittle. Natasha could not endure seeing Katya looking like this. Especially not after last night. The guilt was too much for her; she knew that she had to leave.

"Katya, it might sound silly, but I am homesick."

"It's not silly," said Katya. "Even I still get homesick, once in a while, and this is my home. I can imagine how hard it must have been on you, the last few weeks."

"I've been fine, until lately. I guess it caught up with me, though," Natasha said.

"Natasha, you may leave as soon as you finish my portrait. Is it a deal?"

Natasha gave Katya a big hug. "I love you, my dear Katya."

"I know you do. Otherwise, you would not have done all that you have for me."

There was a knock at the door. Marusia came in with some letters in hand. She gave one to Katya and one to Natasha.

"It's from my mother," said Katya.

"Mine is from Alexander."

"And who is he?" asked Katya.

"A young man I know back home."

"You have been keeping secrets from me. Anyone I know?" Katya asked.

"I think you know him. Dr. Arkadeowitch's son, remember him?"

"Of course. But didn't they move years ago to Odessa?"

"Yes, his parents are still there, but he came back to open his own practice."

"A doctor! And you have never told me. How lucky you are. Is it serious between you two?" Katya asked.

"Well, he is very serious, but I am not," answered Natasha.

"You mean you don't love him?"

"I wish I did."

"What is the matter with him?" asked Katya.

"Nothing. He is a wonderful person. I really don't deserve him."

"Is he still as handsome as he was?"

"Yes, he is. You should see how all the women fawn over him."

"But he loves you, Natasha. He is not interested in the other women. Am I right?"

"He loves me, but I don't love him."

"Of course, it isn't fair," said Katya, talking from experience. "You don't choose the person that you want to fall in love with. You just fall in love. You meet a person, something happens to you, and all of a sudden, you are in love, without having any idea if the other person is in love with you."

"I guess so," agreed Natasha, trying not to think about Grisha.

"Of course I am right. Why don't you quickly rip open the letter and see what he has to say. Maybe he has found someone else," Katya said teasingly.

"Katya, don't be funny."

"I'm just joking. You know that."

"This is very serious," said Natasha.

"Then what are you going to do about him?"

"I don't know yet. I'll wait and see what time will bring."

"Come on. Open the letter. I can't wait to see what he has to say," said Katya, with the eagerness of a young schoolgirl.

"I think I will wait until tonight," Natasha said teasingly.

"You know that I couldn't stand the suspense," Katya said. She watched as Natasha opened the letter and started to read. Katya saw Natasha's smile disappear. "What is wrong?"

"He's leaving," Natasha said gravely disappointed that he would not be home waiting for her.

"You mean he's found somebody new?"

"No, not like that," Natasha said. "He is going to Odessa. His mother passed away."

"Oh, I am truly sorry. I shouldn't have joked like that. Does he say anything else?"

"Only that he will be away at least a fortnight to comfort his father."

"God rest his mother's soul," said Katya.

And Natasha repeated the same.

The next five days went by quietly. Grisha had been away on business. He was expected to return the next day.

As soon as Grisha came back, Natasha told him that she was leaving.

"Why are you leaving so suddenly?" Grisha asked, surprised.

"It isn't all that sudden. I've been thinking about it for some time now," Natasha said, trying to avoid his eyes.

"Does Katya know that you're going?"

"Yes, I told her a few days ago, that, as soon as we were finished with the portrait, I was going home."

Natasha could tell that Grisha was hurt, and that he didn't like the idea of her leaving. But, she had no other choice. She had made up her mind. There was no turning back now. Once she decided something, she always tried to do it.

"I really must go," she said, after seeing how sad Grisha looked. "My mother misses me. And besides, Katya's mother is coming next week to keep her company."

Stopa, who was sitting nearby, said, "We are going to miss you. Are you sure you can't stay?"

"I really must leave. I already wrote home telling them that I will return this week. I really would like to stay, but it is better this way."

Later that night, after she checked to make sure that Katya was all right, Natasha went downstairs. She saw Stopa in the covered greenhouse sitting comfortably and smoking a pipe. She was pleased that it was Stopa and not Grisha. All she was in the mood for was simple talk. She enjoyed talking to Stopa. He always had the right answers and always had time for her. At least, that's what she thought. There was so much that he could have taught her about nature.

"May I join you, Stopa?" Natasha asked.

"Of course, my child. Come and sit next to me and bring cheer to an old man's heart."

She made herself comfortable next to him. The night wasn't as bright and warm as yesterday. It felt as if there were going to be a change in the weather. It was beginning to get windy and brisk.

"Let's hope that we won't get any rain," he said as if guessing what she was thinking. "That is the last thing we need right now, with all the crops still in the fields. We need a few days of good weather in order to bring in the crop.

Natasha could see that he was as concerned with the fields as he was with his own body.

They sat in silence and watched the smoke rings drift up from Stopa's pipe. They both regreteed that they had not spent more time together. It is sad that only when we are about to lose something, do we first come to appreciate it.

Stopa took her hand in his and gave it a squeeze, a squeeze that said that they were friends.

The magic of the moment was broken by Grisha's entrance. He carried three cups and a silver samovar full of hot tea.

"I hope that I am not interrupting anything important?" he asked with a smile.

"Of course not," said Natasha. "We were just talking about the weather. There is plenty of room for all of us." She remained sitting next to Stopa, as Grisha took the chair opposite them. He poured the tea into the cups.

"Natasha," Grisha said. "I saw the finished portrait. It is wonderful. You are a true artist."

"You weren't supposed to see it until tomorrow night," Natasha said angrily. "That is why I covered it."

"It was uncovered when I went in tonight," he said apologetically.

"Oh well, it was finished anyway. But, I wanted it to be a surprise. Tomorrow night, Katya and I planned a big unveiling. She was the one that didn't want anybody to see it before the ceremony."

The three of them sat together for a few moments. Stopa was the first to leave. He said that he had to be up early in the morning. In fact, this was just an excuse. He sensed that Grisha wanted to be alone with Natasha. As Stopa was leaving, Natasha rose at the same time.

"Good night, Grisha. I think that I will retire early, also."

"Can't you stay a little while?" Grisha pleaded. "There is something that I must say to you. It won't take too long, I promise."

Natasha did not want to stay, but she was trapped by her own fear — fear of going and fear of staying. She sat down and held her hands tightly in her lap. He sat beside her.

"Natasha, you are leaving because of what happened between us, aren't you?"

"Not really," she said, without looking at him.

"I don't blame you. I behaved like a fool. Can you ever forgive me?"

"There is nothing to forgive," Natasha said. "It was just as much my fault as yours."

"No, it was all my fault," he insisted. "I am older and I should have known better. You are still a child."

"I am not a child. Don't ever call me that again," Natasha said angrily. "It wasn't anybody's fault. These things just happen."

She wished it were so. But she knew it wasn't true. She wanted to kiss him and hold him now, just as much as she did then. Her whole body ached from having to hold back all the love that he had awakened in her. She wondered why such a beautiful thing as love could never be easy. It seemed to her as if pain were the only unfettered emotion.

"I promise that it will never happen again," Grisha said solemnly.

The finality of his words made her cry. She ran into her room, before he could see the tears. There was not time to say good night.

Natasha fell on her bed and cried. She felt foolish, but she cried anyway. She wished she could fall asleep, but her body was too tense. Scenes from the past days flashed through her mind. She felt young, very young. There was still so much to learn.

Because the rebels had sabotaged the main track, Natasha was forced to postpone her departure. She was not interested in politics, but, nonetheless, politics were influencing her life.

Stopa had gone into town to find out when the blownup track would be repaired, and when normal rail service would resume. Natasha waited anxiously for his return. She sat beneath a large chestnut tree whose roots stretched to the far corners of the back garden. Natasha put down the copy of *Anna Karenina* that she had been reading.

She watched Marusia cleaning the beans for dinner. Natasha had been on good terms with Marusia ever since she arrived. Marusia had been as much a mother to her, as Stopa had been a father. The two women had spent a lot of time together, especially in the evenings, after Katya had fallen asleep. Marusia taught Natasha how to weave. She also taught Natasha the difference between poisonous herbs and medicinal ones.

Marusia began to tell Natasha her life story. She told how she never married, because the only man she loved was killed in a hunting accident. After that, she devoted herself entirely to the Grillow family. They were good to her and treated her like one of the family. She had been with them for thirty years, ever since she was a young girl.

"I was sick and I had no place to go," Marusia said. "Both of my parents died from tuberculosis, and I was left alone. If these good people had not taken me in, I would not be alive today. They nursed me back to health and said that I could live with them if I wanted to. I knew that I was welcome, and so I stayed."

Tears ran down her cheeks as she told Natasha her story. Marusia began humming a sad and melancholy song. Natasha joined in with her. It was an old Russian love song. In the future, whenever Natasha heard that song, she thought of Marusia.

Stopa had come back from town at last. Natasha ran to meet him.

"Good morning, Natasha," he said. "Don't tell me you have been waiting just for me all morning?" Anticipating her question, he told her that the trains would be running again the next day, and that she could take the one leaving at 7:15 at night. Stopa's harried expression betrayed concern. Natasha wondered if there had been more trouble with the rebels.

Natasha had started walking up the stairs to Katya's room, when Stopa came running. "Here Natasha, I have a letter for you. I was in such a hurry I almost forgot to give it to you."

As she reached for the letter, she said, "Is there something wrong, Stopa? You look worried."

"Yes, but nothing that need bother you."

"Tell me, Stopa," she said imploringly.

He came closer to her and whispered, so that none of the peasants would hear, "There are big uprisings in the city."

"How serious is it?" she asked.

"I'm sure that they will quiet down," he reassured her, and then ran off to talk to Grisha.

Natasha went to her room, after she found Katya asleep. Natasha read the letter from her parents. They wanted her to come back as soon as possible, because they feared that she would be caught in the uprisings which were becoming more common everyday.

The official unveiling of Katya's portrait took place that evening. Everyone stood around drinking champagne, as Stopa hung the portrait over the mantlepiece. Natasha had painted a young and vibrant Katya — the Katya whom she remembered from her youth — not the pale and livid Katya who, like a withered husk, had to be supported on Grisha's arm, as she stared wistfully at the sad reminder of her former self.

Natasha spent her last night with Katya in her room. It had been Katya's wish. Natasha lay in the darkness, but a few feet from her friend. The only sound that she could hear was Katya's faint breathing. Natasha imagined that a little bit of Katya's soul was escaping into the air with each breath.

Why do people have to die, she wondered. Especially the young, who are just beginning to live. First, it had been her brothers, and now Katya. Why, she wondered. Why?

She asked the question until she fell asleep. And then she dreamed it.

The next morning Natasha got up early in order to bid good-bye to her favorite places. She took a long walk on the beach and came back just as Katya was waking. She spent most of the day with Katya. There was so much to say, but neither of them could find the words, and so most of the day was spent in silence.

When it came time for Natasha to leave, Grisha carried her bags down to the carriage. Grisha saw the two women facing each other silently in Katya's room. They were too sad to say good-by. And then, there was only Katya, alone, in the room. Alone, except for the doll, which she clutched to her bosom. She squeezed it tightly, as if it were Natasha herself that she was holding. It would not be long now before only the doll would remain in that sad bedroom.

Natasha found herself walking down the long stairs. She held the thick wood railing in order to steady herself. She walked out the main door and closed it behind her.

Natasha and Grisha did not talk much on the way to the station. There was nothing, really, that could be said. They were both glad that the train was on time. They parted the way most people part. Each promised to write to the other. They said their Dosvidanyas. In fact, they said them several times. At the last possible instant, Grisha slipped a small icon depicting the madonna and child into Natasha's hand. Her "thank you" was concealed behind the blast of the train's whistle.

No, their parting was not unusual. There are not many ways to say good-by. At least not for people who really care for each other.

Through her window, Natasha watched Grisha's form grow smaller as the distance between them increased with the speed of the train. Grisha stayed on the platform waving, long after he knew the train was out of sight.

III

Everyone was beaming at the sight of her. Especially her mother, who was sure that the rebels would attack the train again. When they got back to the house, Natasha's mother immediately began telling her all the local gossip that she had missed. But Natasha was not interested now. All that she could think about was Katya. And Grisha too. And Grisha too.

Natasha had hoped that being back home would distract her from the thoughts that plagued her that summer. But it didn't. If anything, it increased them. Everything at home seemed dull and commonplace compared with her experiences of the summer.

After about a week, Natasha's mother began to worry about her. She would ask Natasha what was the matter, but always received the same answer: "I am fine, don't worry about me so much."

Natasha saw Alexander, but only for short periods. When Natasha's mother mentioned this to her husband, he would say: "Just give the girl some time. She is still upset about Katya. She will be fine again soon."

"I should never have let her go," the mother would say, blaming herself.

"Oh, stop thinking such things," the father would reply. "There is nothing wrong with her that a little time won't fix."

"But what about Alexander?" pleaded the mother. "How long do you think he is going to stand for this?"

"Well, maybe it's not such a bad thing. It will give them time to see how they really feel about each other," the father would respond.

"I don't know how you can be that cool about all this," she would persist. "After all, your daughter's future is at stake."

"There is nothing to worry about. Alexander really loves Natasha, and a man in love will endure almost anything."

"I hope you're right, dear," she would say. Then she would return to whatever she was involved with at that moment, only to resurrect the same topic of conversation a little later.

Natasha's feelings about herself were getting much more positive. She thought she was doing pretty well, all things considered. She was busy with her studies, which consumed most of her time. She did not really know just how she felt about Alexander. She thought that if she avoided him, she would soon discover how she really felt about him.

As time passed, she began to think less and less often of Grisha. She was sure that soon she would completely forget him, and her life would return to normal. The only times she knew she was really kidding herself were when she caught a glimpse of her little icon and felt a sudden terrible twinge of loneliness and longing.

Three weeks after her return home, she received the news she had both feared and expected. Katya had died. The letter was from Grisha, of course. It said that he was going on a long trip through Europe. He wrote that he had to get far away, but that he would correspond with her and let her know where he was. Natasha's tears were bitter but few. She found comfort in the thought that Katya's suffering had ended. It had been so hard for her, lingering on all those months with no hope of recovery. It had been so cruel. Life is too beautiful to sit around waiting to say good-by to it. Natasha knew that in the end, she could never be as brave as Katya. She hoped that when it came her turn to die, she would die instantly and unexpectedly.

Sometime later, Natasha and her mother went to visit Katya's mother. When she saw them, Mrs. Suputenko's composure broke and she began sobbing. She was wearing mourning clothes, which she continued to wear until she herself died some years later.

As they sipped tea, the broken woman told them about Katya's last days. "Katya became so weak that she could not even speak, let alone move any part of her body," she told them.

Natasha sat motionless in the chair, and listened to every word. Katya's mother motioned for Natasha to come sit next to her on the sofa. She reached beneath her and pulled out Katya's doll, and handed it to Natasha. With new tears and a trembling voice, she said, "Katya wanted you to have this."

Natasha could no longer control herself, and she let her tears come without restraint.

When they returned home later that day, Natasha went straight to her room and placed the doll in its rightful place, next to the icon. It did not even occur to Natasha that Grisha was now free. If anything, she thought more of Alexander.

The next two months passed easily, bringing with them, two letters from Grisha. They both came from different places, with no specified return address, eliminating any responsibility to answer them.

The hours that Natasha spent with Alexander brought him closer to her. Soon, she even looked forward to seeing him. But she still did not know if she was merely happy with him, or if she really loved him. His cheerfulness was contagious, and affected everyone around him. It was easy to talk to him. He still continued to ask for her hand in marriage.

"Why wait until you finish your studies?" he would say. "You can finish when we are married."

"No, we are going to wait, just as we originally agreed to do," Natasha insisted.

"OK, you win. You are a stubborn girl. I don't know why I put up with you," he would tease her. Then he would take her into his arms and gently kiss her in a brotherly way. But he was a patient man, and he also knew that the day would come when Natasha was going to want him as much as he wanted her. Their future still lay ahead.

The winter came and the snow covered everything in sight. The winter made the small houses appear even smaller. The branches of the trees were heavy with pounds of snow. The streets were filled with children having snow battles. Sad and happy snowmen appeared everywhere, and every hill was filled with sleds.

Winter gave everyone a rest from the long and hard work of bringing in the summer harvest. It was snowing slightly, as Natasha and Alexander walked to church one winter night. As they approached the church, they could hear the choir singing. The church steeple glittered with frozen icicles.

When they were praying inside, Natasha glanced at Alexander. It surprised her that such a strong man could look so meek and humble. She felt proud that he loved her. But she felt guilty, also. Guilty at not being able to return his love. She began to pray, and her prayers asked God to make her love Alexander. If only that were so, life would be so wonderful. She gazed at Alexander again, trying to convince herself that she really loved him.

Alexander caught her glance this time and held it. He probed deep into her eyes. For an instant, he saw what he was sure was love. The sight warmed his heart.

Natasha laid her small hand gently inside his large one. She looked up at him. He smiled, and she returned the smile. Then, he led her outside into the snow.

The night was unbelievably crisp and beautiful. Everything was frozen, including the night itself. Nothing moved; everything was as silent as the light coming in through the patterned windows. The choir could be heard behind them. What a wonderful night. The whole world seemed at peace. They walked for a long time, crunching the soft snow beneath their boots. Natasha looked charming in her white fur cap and muff. Alexander felt proud to be with her, but, at the same time, was uneasy. He felt something was bothering Natasha.

"What is wrong, dear?" he asked, after a long silence.

"What do you mean?" she said, not feeling yet like revealing her heart to him.

"You are so quiet tonight. What is the matter?"

"I don't know. I really don't know," she insisted.

"But, there must be something. Otherwise, you would not be so quiet."

They walked on in silence. Then he broke the silence again.

"May I guess at what is the matter?"

Natasha frowned, but did not refuse.

"Is it something about us?"

She looked away abruptly.

"Come on. You can tell me, my love," he said, as he put his arm around her shoulder.

Natasha searched for the right words. She wanted to tell him the truth, but she did not want to hurt him. He was so fine and good.

"Let me help you," Alexander said. "I think I know what is bothering you."

"How can you know?" she said, as she stared at him.

"I know, my dear, I can feel it. I have felt it coming. You are going to tell me that you don't love me. Am I right?"

She was afraid to answer. Finally she said, "Was it really so obvious?"

"Oh, Natasha, I have known that there was something wrong, ever since you came back from Katya's. I kept hoping that it was only sorrow for Katya, but now I think that you have fallen in love with someone else."

"Of course not," she answered indignantly. "It is just that I am unsure whether or not I really love you. I don't even know what love really is. I want to, Alexander. But I am still so unsure. I don't deserve you. There are so many other women who would give you more love than I ever could give."

"That is not so," he said.

Natasha continued, as if she hadn't heard him. "I won't make you happy. You deserve so much more. You are so wonderful."

"No, Natasha. Only you can make me happy," he said, pleadingly. "I don't want anybody else. I will wait for you until you do want me."

He watched the snowflakes settle gently on her eyelashes. Then he took her into his arms and kissed her eyes until the snowflakes melted. Then he kissed her hard on the lips. She did not resist, and, for the first time, returned his kiss. For a minute, the world turned about them. He wanted to kiss her again, but she stepped back a little and said:

"You shouldn't do that. It makes me so confused."

"That's exactly why I did it," he said. "As long as you don't love someone else, I am going to keep trying to make you love me. In the meantime, I love you enough for the two of us."

A man came by, and, suddenly, they were no longer alone. Arm in arm, they strolled further down the path.

It feels so good when I am with him, Natasha thought. Maybe, after we are married, I will learn to love him. She glanced up at the stars for a moment and watched them sparkle. Then, she looked down at the new snow and watched it sparkle, too. Snow is made up of fallen stars, she thought. Then she looked at Alexander. Strong, handsome Alexander. It felt so good to be with a man. A real man. It was at that moment that she made up her mind to marry him.

She stopped abruptly in the middle of the road, pulled her hand out of the muff, and then stretched her whole body up so that her lips could meet his. There was no response from him. It all happened so fast. For a moment, he was surprised. Then, he took her up into his strong arms and kissed her passionately. She forgot everything in his embrace. All her doubts vanished as they stood in the middle of the deserted road and found their world in each other. Natasha felt the words, "I love you," rising within her. She wanted to say them, but she couldn't. She said instead, "I am willing to marry, if you will have me."

He picked her up and swung her about in his excitement. He sang at the top of his voice, "I love you. I love you." He wanted the whole world to know. "You won't be sorry, Natasha, I promise you."

"I will try to be a good wife and to make you happy," Natasha said in calm contrast.

Although he did not hear the words he longed so much to hear, Alexander was still overwhelmingly happy. Just the chance that she would love him one day was good enough for him. Every man has his obsession; Alexander had his Natasha.

"Let's tell mamma and pappa the news tonight," she said, as they walked through the gate of her house. "I am sure that they will be delighted to know."

Natasha's parents were, indeed, thrilled, and her mother began making detailed plans for the wedding. Natasha interrupted her, "Mother, the wedding is a whole year off. Don't you think the wedding list can wait a while."

"I guess so," the mother conceded. "But you don't want to let things go until the last minute."

Alexander then began to play a game of chess with Natasha's father. It looked, already, as if he were a member of the family. The wedding would only make it official.

Winter was on its way out and spring moved in, bringing the slushy, dirty mess with it. Gray skies, muddy roads, and frequent puddles characterized the transition period. And then, all at once, it was really spring. The soft petals of the flowers broke through the hard ground, and the birds returned from wherever they had been. The fields were being plowed now and made ready for the spring planting. The farmers' wives could be seen bending over their new vegetable gardens. There was activity everywhere. The miracle of spring infused Natasha with a new sense of life and hope. In the weeks that followed, Natasha and Alexander did not see much of each other. Natasha was busy with her studies, and Alexander was consumed by his medical duties, since he was the town's only doctor.

Alexander had been raised in wealth and comfort, but this only seemed to make him more willing to break his back for little or no money. He lived in the old family house. Its exterior showed some signs of neglect because Alexander's parents had not bothered to keep it up. Two downstairs rooms of the house served as the examining and waiting rooms. Alexander himself was not wealthy, and his patients were poor and slow paying. A good deal of his payment came in the form of services, rather than money. There was a woman who did his laundry because her husband was an invalid and needed constant doctor's care. His gardener was also an impoverished patient. He had been tending the grounds for months now. Alexander told him to stop coming, because he had already worked off the debt. But he refused and kept coming anyway. The peasant women rarely came for a visit without bringing him some kind of baked goods. He felt rich, even without money. And now that he would have Natasha, he had everything he could possibly want.

Whenever Natasha had free time, she would help him with his practice. He loved those days when they worked side by side. Natasha could not stand the sight of blood, however. It made her faint.

"I think I never could be a nurse," she confessed to him one day.

"I feel the pain more than the patients. It took me a long time to get used to it, too," Alexander said, trying to soothe her.

Alexander's poverty came to an abrupt end when he received a telegram notifying him of the settlement of his mother's estate. He told Natasha as soon as he heard.

"Now I can buy all the modern equipment that I need," he said.

"Yes, and you'll be able to afford a full-time nurse, instead of a bungler like me."

"But, you're a very special bungler," he said, as he embraced her.

"Be sure to be on time tonight," Natasha said, as she was leaving for home. "Father is anxious to finish that chess game that you started yesterday."

"Tell him not to be so anxious. I feel that this time, at least, I am going to come out on top."

"I'll see you later, darling," she said.

"Yes, and don't forget that I love you," he exclaimed, as she closed the door.

Natasha had become completely attached to Alexander. They experienced moments of great happiness together. Now, she no longer had to decide to make him happy. It had become a natural act of giving.

Eight months had passed since Katya had died and Grisha had left for Europe. He had written to Natasha that he could not return to Russia just yet, because the memories were still too painful. He enjoyed meeting strangers. Familiar faces depressed him. Natasha wrote him back at the Italian address that was on the envelope. She encouraged him to return home quickly, because it would be impossible to forget Katya by just running away. After that, the correspondence ended. For months, she did not know where he was or how he was.

And then the summer came—a beautiful Russian summer. It seemed as if there were more of everything in the summer—more dancing, more fun, and even more time.

Natasha had a break from her studies. She decided to spend it doing a painting of one of her favorite spots. She walked along a twisting creek, which, though frozen all winter, now rippled along just as it had the summer before. She could see Katya's family house in the distance. It was all white and surrounded by a white fence. On the north side of the creek were rolling hills, covered with birch trees. Their black and white bark looked like pure silver in the distance. Natasha loved this place. There was tall grass on both sides of the stream, as tall as Natasha herself. She stood for a while under the big weeping willow, which Katya had loved so much. They had spent hours together, holding on to the willow's long vines and swinging across the stream. Occasionally, a vine would break, and one of them would fall in, to the great amusement of the other.

As she worked on her painting, she felt as much a part of the scenery as the trees that she painted. She wore a blue ribbon in her hair, which matched exactly the sky above.

While Natasha was painting peacefully, a visitor knocked on the door of her house. The maid answered the door and showed the gentleman in.

"May I present Grisha Grillow," the maid announced to Natasha's father.

Mr. Borisovna paused for a second, trying to place the name. Then he remembered.

"My dear Grisha, what a wonderful surprise," he said in welcome.

Grisha followed Natasha's father into the sitting room, where Natasha's mother was sipping afternoon tea.

"What a pleasant surprise," she said. "How nice it is to see you again." She purposely did not mention Katya.

"Maria Ivanovna," Grisha replied, "thank you so much."

"Grisha, why didn't you write us and tell us that you intended to come to visit us? We would have picked you up at the station," chided Mr. Borisovna.

"I didn't have the time to write," Grisha said. "I'm here on business, and was not certain that I would have the time to drop in."

"We are very sorry about Katya's death," Mr. Borisovna said. "It must be very hard on you."

"Yes, it is very hard to live without her," Grisha admitted.

"Did you walk all the way from the station?" Mr. Borisovna asked, trying to change the subject.

"Yes, the walk did me good," Grisha responded. "I enjoyed

it and it gave me an opportunity to see the town once more."

"But you must be exhausted from your trip. Would you like some tea?" asked Natasha's mother.

"Maybe Grisha would like to have something stronger," interrupted Mr. Borisovna.

"Thank you, but I would prefer some tea." Grisha had never cared for liquor.

"Are you planning to stay long?" Mrs. Borisovna asked as she poured the tea.

"I don't really know yet," he said noncommitally. "It all depends how long my business takes to complete."

"Natasha will be thrilled to see you," said Mrs. Borisovna.

Natasha was the real reason that Grisha was in the neighborhood, though he did not want to reveal this to her family.

"If you decide not to stay with Katya's parents, you are, of course, welcome to stay with us," Mrs. Borisovna said.

"I would prefer to stay here, if it would not be too much trouble for you."

"It's no trouble at all," said Mr. Borisovna.

"You know, of course, that Natasha is going to be married in two months," Maria Ivanovna said.

"Yes, she wrote me about the news," Grisha said and tried to sound happy for her.

"Natasha was very worried when you didn't answer her letter," Mr. Borisovna said.

Talk of Natasha made Grisha's heart pound faster. He couldn't wait to see her, because seeing her would be like seeing Katya again.

"Where is Natasha?" Grisha asked, trying to appear nonchallant.

"She is down by the stream," Maria Ivanovna said. "She promised to be back in time for tea, but when she is painting, she loses track of time."

"Do you think that it would be a good idea if I went down and surprised her?" Grisha asked.

"That's a wonderful idea. Why don't you do that," agreed Mr. Borisovna before his wife had time to object.

Grisha tried to walk slowly, but his feet would not cooperate.

He did not want Natasha to notice how anxious he was. He came to the top of a steep hill and saw her standing down below. She was standing by her easel. He remained silent for a while, not wanting to disturb her. She didn't notice him, until she looked up to see how high the sun was. She saw a man, but, at first, could not tell who it was. Finally, when her eyes discerned his identity, her mind still refused to believe it. No, it can't be him, she thought. Grisha is still someplace in Europe. Then she heard him calling her name. She dropped everything and ran to him. They met half-way up the hill and fell into each other's arms. Holding him close, her eyes filled with tears of happiness. She forgot Alexander completely. The only thing that mattered to her now was that she was in the arms of the man that she really loved.

"I am so glad to see you," she said tenderly.

"But not as glad as I am to see you," he said.

He stepped back and he took a good long look at her.

"You are even more beautiful than I remembered," he said.

"Thank you," she said blushing. "How are you and how did you get here?" Natasha asked, combining all her questions. How come you didn't write for such a long time? I have been so worried."

"I'm fine now that I see you. I am sorry if I have made you worry. I just wanted to be alone and away from things that reminded me of Katya. And you make me think of her more than anything else.

Natasha felt happy, happier than she had felt for months. And then she remembered Alexander. Poor Alexander. With this thought, the expression on her face soured. She shook her head back and forth.

"What is the matter?" Grisha asked, noticing the change in her face.

"The matter?" she asked.

"You are so sad," he said. "You are going to be married, soon. That should make you happy."

"Of course I am happy. I have no reason not to be. I am going to be married to the most wonderful man in the world. A man that loves me very much. I have everything that a normal girl would want."

"But what about you?" Grisha asked. "Are you a normal girl?"

Natasha ignored his question and suggested that they begin to walk home. She was not yet ready for him to know the truth.

Grisha had been hoping to find a sad girl, whose life was as unfulfilled as his own. He wanted her to tell him that she was unhappy about her forthcoming marriage. He was disappointed when she did not reveal this to him.

Grisha helped her carry her easel and paints. Talking and laughing, they entered the house. Natasha's parents were waiting for them in the study.

Natasha volunteered to show Grisha to the guest room before her mother could say anything to the contrary. He followed her upstairs to the guest room, which was formerly her brothers' room.

After he changed out of his traveling clothes, Grisha went downstairs, where he found the whole family relaxing in the garden. Natasha was sitting on a swing, humming a song. He sat down in the chair farthest from Natasha, desiring not to arouse any suspicions. The family listened spellbound, as Grisha described the far-off European cities that he had visited.

It was a lovely night. The whole area was permeated by the sweet smell of honeysuckle. Only once in a while did Natasha remember Alexander.

Natasha's mother and father plied Grisha with questions, while she listened in silence. Grisha glanced at her whenever he thought it was safe. She looked particularly beautiful now in a low-cut green dress. Whenever their eyes met, she would blush and look down. It was hard for Grisha to concentrate. Many times he had to force himself not to look her way.

"Grisha, do you play chess?" Mr. Borisovna eventually asked.

"Yes, sir, but not very well."

"How about a game now?" the father proposed.

"Certainly, if you don't mind poor competition," Grisha said.

"It will be a welcome change," the old man said. "Alexander, my future son-in-law, never lets me win."

"That is not true," Natasha interjected. "You win most of the games, and you know it."

Before the game could get started, however, dinner was announced. Mr. Borisovna led the way into the dining room. Grisha took his place opposite Natasha. Her father said grace, and the meal commenced.

Throughout the meal, Natasha and Grisha kept glancing at each other in a manner that indicated more than a casual friendship. Mrs. Borisovna noticed this, and it upset her. She did not want anything to happen now to interfere with the wedding that she so much wanted. Therefore, in order to counteract what she thought was happening, she periodically brought up Alexander's name throughout the meal.

"Where is Alexander?" she would say. "Why has he not come to dinner?"

"Mother," said Natasha, "have you forgotten that he told you he was going to stay with Mrs. Karmoshenko? She is in labor now. You remember how much trouble she had with her last child. Alexander thought that it would not be safe to leave her with just a midwife."

During dessert, the talk turned to Grisha's stay in Paris.

"I would love to see Paris someday," Mrs. Borisovna said. "The way that you describe it, Grisha, it sounds so beautiful."

"I fear that if the present rebellions persist, you might be seeing it sooner than you like," Mr. Borisovna said, to the great consternation of his wife.

Natasha knew better than to even look at her mother.

"Come, Grisha, and I will show you how beautiful the garden looks in the moonlight," Natasha said.

Side by side with Grisha, Natasha walked the familiar path that led into the garden. It seemed to Natasha that the stars above were more numerous and much brighter than she had ever seen them before. And Natasha, herself, felt more alive at this moment than she could ever remember. There was a new moon out, whose silvery brightness lit the way for the two strollers.

"I promised you that I would show you my favorite spot," Natasha said proudly, "and now I am going to do just that."

Soon they came to a spot that was surrounded by oak trees. The trees were planted far enough apart so that their branches could stretch out to their full length. It was like walking under a canopy of leaves, each of which was lit by a moonbeam.

In the distance stood a round garden pavillion. The pavillion was white and surrounded by red roses. The roses were curtained by the darkness, but their sweet fragrance was unmistakable. It was a windless night and a magical one.

"I can easily see why this is your favorite place," Grisha said. "But it is no more beautiful than the woman who shows it to me."

Natasha felt the blood rise to her cheeks, as she thanked him for the compliment. She ran up the stairs of the pavillion. Grisha remained standing below, as Natasha stood between the columns and looked out into the night. He delighted in the grace of her movements, which reminded him so much of Katya.

Natasha wished that the present moment could be frozen in time. The woman in her knew what was coming; the little girl in her wished that the inevitable could be postponed forever.

"You are still afraid of me, aren't you, Natasha?" Grisha said, sensing her trepidation. "Afraid of me even after everything that we've been through together."

"I am not afraid," she said. "But I think that we had better go in now before mother comes after us."

"It is too nice a night to spend inside," he said.

When Grisha saw that Natasha was not going to come down, he went up the stairs and took a seat beside her in the pavillion. The only sound that disturbed the night was the occasional croaking of the frogs, and the intermittent rush of the flowing stream.

Natasha hated herself for resisting him like a child. She knew that she loved him, and that there was nothing wrong with such a love. And yet, she still held back, and for a moment wished that Alexander had come that evening so that she would not have been placed in this position.

"Natasha, are you really in love with Alexander?" Grisha said, asking the question that Natasha dreaded.

"Of course I am," she said. "We are going to be married."

And then her eyes filled with tears, and she began to cry uncontrollably.

"That's just what I thought," he said. Grisha took her face between his hands and turned her head until their eyes met. "I didn't think that I would ever be able to love somebody other than Katya. But I love you," he said suddenly. "Will you marry me?"

For Natasha, it was like hearing churchbells on a Sunday morning. There could be no holding back now. She was ready to give her heart freely and without reservation. His lips were warm and exciting as he kissed her. This time, she did not shiver or try to move away. There was nothing now that she had to hide or be afraid of.

Grisha was overjoyed when she whispered that she loved him also. "If I had found out that you were truly happy with Alexander," he told her, "then I would not have interfered. Though I could never be happy without you, I value your happiness more than mine."

The mention of Alexander's name brought Natasha suddenly back to her senses. She was still engaged to him, and yet, she had just confessed her love to another man. Well, she decided, Alexander will simply have to be told the truth. She knew how much it would hurt him, but there was no other way. Then she thought about her parents, and the wedding plans, and all the people that knew about the engagement.

"Will they think that I have gone mad?" she asked Grisha.

"Don't worry," he reassurred her. "We will explain it to them together."

The kisses that followed were passionate and wild. It seemed as if the flowers, the trees, and even the sky above were joining in their embrace.

When they separated finally, Grisha noticed tears in Natasha's eyes.

"Darling, have I said something wrong?" he asked.

"No, no, no," she replied.

"But, why the tears? Have I done something?"

"No."

"I don't understand," he said.

"It's just that I am so happy, so wonderfully happy."

He swung her around and they danced to a waltz that they pretended to hear. They turned and turned with the bright moon watching them and Natasha's dress flowing in the light evening breeze.

"Let's get married right away," he said. "I don't want to be alone another day. I promise that we will be happy together."

"But we must wait at least two more months, darling."

"Why?" he asked.

"Because I want to finish my studies," she answered.

"If you insist, then I guess I can wait two months. Then, I should return to Soshi in a few days. The estate business cannot be neglected for so long a time. But the next two months will seem like an endless void, without your presence at my side."

Natasha and Grisha walked back to the house arm in arm. They entered the brightly lit sitting room and found Natasha's parents exactly where they had left them. When Natasha saw her parents' peaceful faces, she whispered to Grisha that it would probably be better to wait a few days before telling them.

"Do you really think that would be wise?" he argued. "It will be very hard for me to stay away from you. They will find out sooner or later anyway."

"I guess you are right," she conceded.

Before Grisha could say anything, however, Mr. Borisovna said, "How about that game of chess now? It is still early."

"Gospodin Borisovna, there is something I must ask you first," Grisha said.

Mr. Borisovna, meanwhile, started setting up the chess pieces and was totally unprepared for the coming shock.

"Gospodin Borisovna, I would like to ask for Natasha's hand in marriage."

Without looking at Grisha, Mr. Borisovna got up and went over to Natasha, who was hiding behind a big blue chair.

"Is this some kind of a joke?" he asked, shouting louder than she had ever heard him before. His plump body rippled with waves of indignation.

Seeing the anger on her father's face, she went over to Grisha. He took her trembling hand in his.

"Father, it is no joke," she said finally. "I love Grisha very much, and he is the only one I love."

In the excitement, no one noticed Mr. Borisovna. She had fainted from the shock, and her stout body lay slumped in a chair. The emotional conversation continued.

"What about Alexander?" Mr. Borisovna reminded Natasha.

"But father, I don't love him," Natasha said.

"You have no right to do this to him," the father said in a raised voice. The veins on his forehead bulged with rage.

"He will understand, father. He knows that I don't love him."

"I don't understand my own child!" he said, and dropped weakly into a chair.

"Please, father," Natasha pleaded as she fell down on her knees in front of him. "Don't make this any harder than it already is."

Regaining consciousness, Natasha's mother asked in a daze, "What is the meaning of all of this?"

After Mrs. Borisovna regained her composure, Natasha said, "Mother, I want your blessing in marrying Grisha."

"What about sweet Alexander?" the mother said. "How can you do this shameful thing to him?"

"But mother, you have always been so understanding. How come it is so hard for you to understand me now? Mother, I love Grisha. I have loved him ever since I was a child."

"You are still a child," Mr. Borisovna said coldly. "You don't know what you are doing."

"I know what I am doing, father. I am very sure that Grisha is the man whom I want to marry."

"Child, how could you do this to us?" Mrs. Borisovna said. "The arrangements have all been made for the wedding. What are the people going to say. I will never be able to face them." She began to wipe her eyes with the soft sleeve of her lace handkerchief.

"Nonsense, mother, we live in modern times. People understand now."

"What does that have to do with it," asked her father. "You still are hurting a wonderful man, a man who loves you very much."

"I know that I am going to hurt him, but it is better that it happen now than later. This way, he still has a chance for the happiness which he deserves. And, besides, you always told me to make sure and marry for love."

Her parents were quiet, too shocked to say anything. Natasha continued.

"And so, this is what I want. I know this is right."

"But child, it is wrong," Mrs. Borisovna said sternly. "It has been less than a year since Katya died. What has gotten into you? I did not raise you to act like this."

"Katya would understand," Natasha said. "Believe me, mother, I really tried to forget Grisha. That was the reason why I waited so long in giving Alexander my answer. I would have gone through with the marriage, if Grisha had not come back. Do you understand, mother? I really didn't plan all of this. And, I certainly didn't intend to hurt anyone."

"I understand, my child," Mr. Borisovna said. "But there are going to be so many people hurt."

"The only person who is going to be hurt is Alexander, and that makes me sad. But, father, this way I am giving him a chance to find a woman who really loves him. Father, please give us your blessing!" Natasha was crying now. The tears rolled down her cheeks like little diamonds.

"Well, children, what can I do or say? I want my child to be happy, and if this is how she wants it, I have no choice but to give you my blessing." Natasha's father could not stand to see his daughter cry.

"Father, thank you," she kissed him and went over to her mother.

"Mother, you won't be sorry. Thank you, my dear *mamuchka*."

The men shook hands, and then they both celebrated with a glass of vodka. Mr. Borisovna wasn't all that displeased about his daughter's choice. After all, Grisha was a rich landowner, and much better off than the Borisovna family itself. And so, it was settled.

Natasha could not sleep that night. She was still too excited from the night's events, and too scared at the thought of facing

Alexander the next day. She pictured his face, and she knew how much it was going to hurt him.

Natasha went to see Alexander early the next morning. Alexander's office was full of patients. She ignored the patients, with whom she usually conversed, and walked into the living room. She told the nurse to have Alexander come and see her as soon as he was free.

As she looked around the big dark room, she remembered all the plans that they had made to improve the house. She stared at the self-portrait that she had given him as a Christmas present. Beneath the painting was a vase of flowers, which Alexander changed everyday.

She hoped that he would hurry. She did not know how much longer she would have the courage to tell him. She opened a window and let some light into the dreary room. This was going to have been her home. She tried to repress these troublesome thoughts. If only the situation had not gone as far as it had. She hated herself for leading Alexander on. If only she had listened before more to her heart and less to her mind. She would not have committed herself to marriage to Alexander.

Finally, the door opened, and Alexander came in. He looked as handsome as ever and greeted her with the warm smile that she knew so well. She was startled by his actual presence and, for an instant, forgot why she had come.

"I am sorry, my love, that you had to wait. Nikolai Anakhov caught his hand in a thresher. I thought for a while that I would have to amputate."

"How is he now?" Natasha asked.

"He will be fine, eventually. But now he is very bad off. His family is going to have to do all the harvesting without him this year."

"I feel sorry for them," Natasha said.

"Don't you want to know what Mrs. Fredowna had?"

"Oh, I forgot all about her. Yes, what did she have?"

"A son, a big eight-pound." Alexander answered.

"Wonderful! That's what they wanted," Natasha said.

Alexander came closer, took her into his arms, and tried to

kiss her. But Natasha pushed free of his embrace.

"Alexander, there is something very unpleasant that I must tell you."

She stepped back and tried to tell him, but no words came. She went to the window and stared out, as if she were trying to read the words on the street below. Her eyes were full of tears, and she could barely see in front of her. Then she felt his hands around her waist.

"What is it, my sweet?" he asked.

She still couldn't talk.

"Why are you crying? What is it?" he said tenderly.

She didn't say anything and he continued to hold her.

"Don't cry. It can't be all that bad," he said finally. He wiped away the tears that were running down her cheeks.

"I have something bad to tell you," she repeated.

"Something about us?" he said. At last, he was getting some sense of the situation.

"Yes."

"What is it?" he asked in his understanding way.

"I can't marry you," she said quickly, trying to get the words out before she choked with tears.

He let her go and walked over to where her portrait was hanging. He looked up at the portrait and talked to it as if he were talking to Natasha herself.

"I never believed that the marriage would really take place. It was too good to be true," he told the picture. As he spoke, tears began dropping from his eyes onto the flowers below.

"I am very sorry to hurt you this way," she said, staring at his hunched back. She could feel the pain that he was suffering.

"I know that," he said. "And that's what makes me most sad."

They both remained silent for a while.

"Are you in love with someone else?" he finally said.

"Yes."

"Someone I know?"

"Yes, Grisha Grillow."

"So, it is Grisha. I knew that there was someone else."

"I am truly sorry. Try not to hate me too much," Natasha said.

"How could I ever hate you?"

"Please forgive me for hurting you this way," she begged him.

"There is nothing to forgive," he said patiently. "The important thing now is for you to be happy. And if you think that he is the one that will make you happy, then I don't want to stand in your way."

He walked over to her and kissed her trembling hands.

"If you ever need me, Natasha, I'll always be here waiting for you."

He held her hands tight now, not wanting to let them go. He knew that once she left his house, she would be out of his life forever. And then she pulled away, and he could not stop her.

As she walked along the old familiar streets, everything seemed different. She took the long way home, hoping to lose some of the guilt on the way. She passed her father's store and, on an impulse, decided to go in. It was a large store, which carried mostly hardware and household goods, along with some gift items. She looked around for something special to bring Grisha. At first, she could not find anything suitable. Then she saw a small handmade gold cross. She had it wrapped and then went straight home.

It was still early in the day, but the humidity was high, and the weather was uncomfortable. Grisha was away doing some errands, and so Natasha decided to go for a swim in the meantime.

She swam a few strokes in the cool stream, and then wrapped herself in a large linen sheet. She lay beside the stream and watched a bee descend onto a red poppy which had just opened from the heat. She felt better now. Her life seemed more honest. She shut her eyes and enjoyed the feel of the sun. Everything had happened so quickly it seemed like a dream. She lay there, afraid to open her eyes and find out differently. She thought about Grisha, and the thoughts warmed her body even more. She wasn't ashamed about her feelings any longer. She felt free, free to be a woman.

Then she felt a shadow over her. She opened her eyes and saw Grisha standing there. He sat down next to her and silently admired her beauty.

"Did you speak to Alexander?" he asked.

"Yes," she replied. "It's all settled."

"You don't sound totally pleased."

"I am," Natasha said, "but I still feel sorry for Alexander. He is a true gentleman."

"That he is," Grisha agreed.

Grisha tried to slide his hand under the sheet which covered Natasha's breasts. She jerked away suddenly, and this greatly surprised Grisha.

"Not here, and not now," Natasha said firmly. "Let us go back to the house now."

Grisha followed close behind, as Natasha led the way home.

They spent a quiet evening at home. Maria Ivanovna examined the wedding plans. Natasha read Turgenev's *Fathers and Sons*, and Grisha played several games of chess with Mr. Borisovna.

Natasha awoke late the next day. When she came down, it was almost eleven o'clock. Grisha was sitting with her mother in the garden.

"Good morning, mother," she said and kissed her on the cheek, "Good morning, Grisha." She sat down next to him.

"Child, you must be starved," the mother said.

"No, mother, I just had my breakfast. Or perhaps I should say, lunch."

The three of them chatted a few moments. Soon, Maria Ivanovna, sensing the fact that the two young people wanted to be alone, politely excused herself.

After Natasha's mother had left, Grisha said, "Darling, you look simply stunning in red." The look in his eyes showed that he meant his words.

"It is my father's favorite color, too," she said.

"From now on, everything that you will get from me will be red."

They spent the rest of the day laughing and talking together. They talked until the sun collapsed beneath the horizon, leaving a stream of fiery color to applaud its departure. The sun was setting as they sat under a big oak tree and discussed each and every detail of the forthcoming wedding.

"Natasha, I have a present for you," Grisha said. He handed her a small blue velvet box.

She opened the box slowly, as if she expected a butterfly to fly out. Inside was a string of white pearls — the most beautiful pearls that Natasha had ever seen. Grisha fastened them around Natasha's neck and then kissed her gently on the forehead. Natasha was too overcome with joy to say anything. All she could think of that night were the pearls, the sunset, and Grisha.

The next morning, right before Grisha's train left for the south, Natasha presented him with her own gift. He did not open the gift-wrapped package until the train was under way.

As he tore off the wrapping, Grisha remembered Natasha's words: "Here is something to remind you of me and to keep you safe." He was delighted to see the small gold cross. He kissed it, put it around his neck, and let it rest against his heart. It would remain there for the rest of his life.

The next two months passed quickly. Natasha was kept busy finishing her studies, while her mother took responsibility for the wedding plans. The only thing that Natasha concerned herself with was the wedding trousseau. Natasha did not want a big wedding, but her mother would not even consider a small affair.

The smell of autumn was in the air, and children baked potatoes in the burning leaves. Natasha rarely saw Alexander. When they did meet, they would greet each other politely and pass on their separate ways. Natasha had heard, from Alexander's nurse, that he had been very depressed lately. It was even rumored that he was neglecting his patients because of overdrinking. This worried Natasha, but there was really nothing that she could do about it.

Grisha's letters increased in number as the wedding day approached. Not a day would go by without Natasha's receiving a little present from him. He had even arranged for somebody in town to present Natasha with flowers everyday.

Autumn finally arrived. A cold wind blew across the harvested fields and ripped at the dried leaves that still hung on the almost bare trees. Grisha arrived two days before the wedding. All was in readiness for the big day.

IV

The wedding day was warm, despite the fall chill. Natasha
got up early. She took a hot bath, experimented with hair
styles, and tried to stay calm. She had hardly seen Grisha
during the last two days. Her mother insisted that this was
proper procedure for the wedding couple. Natasha didn't
argue with her.

Natasha was pleased with her reflection in the full-length
mirror. The magestic silk organza gown fit her perfectly. It fell
softly down her hips, and its train draped gently behind her.

"Tamara, I will miss you," Natasha said to the young
woman who made the dress.

"I will miss you, too, Natasha," the seamstress said, getting
up from the floor.

"I will never find another seamstress as good as you."

"It was easy with a figure like yours," Tamara said. "I
enjoyed making dresses for you."

"Thank you, Tamara," Natasha said, putting her arms
around the seamstress.

"You look simply magnificent," Tamara told her, as she
helped her to put on the floor length veil. It was a cherished
heirloom from Natasha's maternal line. The handmade lace
had not discolored with the generations.

"Thank you. Are you sure that I look all right? Oh, I am so
happy. I only hope that I won't start crying when I get to
church," Natasha said nervously.

"You won't. You just keep your mind on Grisha, and you
will be fine," the seamstress advised.

"Are you coming to church, Tamara?"

"I wouldn't miss it for anything in the world."

"Come on, child. It's time to leave," Natasha's father said
anxiously. "Everyone is waiting downstairs."

When Natasha came down, the family and its close friends
were already lined up in their decorated carriages, waiting for

the bride. As the carriage pulled away, crisp golden brown leaves crackled beneath the wheels.

It seemed as if the whole town was outside the church trying to get a look at the bride. Natasha smiled as she passed them. The small children threw flowers at her feet, and the old women whispered about how beautiful she looked.

The church itself was crowded with friends and family. Everyone turned his head, as she came down the long aisle beside her father. Natasha kept her eyes firmly on Grisha. A thousand candles lit her entrance. There was a piercing stillness that seemed likely to shatter the stained glass windows.

It was a beautiful picture. Women cried, as they saw her walking down the aisle with a simple wreath of wild flowers on her head. The long veil blew gently, as she walked towards the altar. Never for an instant did she take her eyes off Grisha. Their trembling hands touched, and together they walked down the aisle to where the priest was waiting.

The services lasted about an hour. As Natasha was leaving arm in arm with Grisha, she saw Alexander huddled in the darkness against the back wall of the church. Their eyes met, and she knew that she could not leave without speaking to him. While Grisha thanked the guests for coming, Natasha walked over to Alexander.

"Alexander, I am so glad to see you," Natasha said. "Your presence here has made me very happy." Tears filled her eyes.

"You look lovely," he said. "I know that you will be happy with . . ." Before Alexander could complete the sentence, Grisha walked up. "Take good care of her," Alexander said as he shook Grisha's hand and then hurried from the church.

After the banquet, Grisha and Natasha went out and threw handfuls of change to the children. This was an old Russian custom, which signified that the couple would always have plenty left over to give to the poor. The children fought among themselves for each coin that was thrown. Afterward everybody joined hands and danced in the street. The newlyweds shook hands with all their friends. It was a day that nobody could easily forget, especially Natasha.

"Darling, there is something I have to tell you," Grisha said, when he and Natasha were finally alone. "I am afraid that you will not like what I must say."

"What is it?" Natasha asked, startled by the change in mood.

"We will have to leave here tonight."

"But, why?" Natasha asked.

"There is some trouble that started before I came here. We have no choice but to leave at once."

"But why didn't you tell me about it before?" Natasha said.

"I didn't want to spoil the day for you," Grisha said.

Natasha's parents were disturbed by the change in plans. They did not expect Natasha to go so far away from them so soon. Lala was told to pack Natasha's things at once, but only the most essential ones. The rest would be sent after their departure.

The train was full all the way to Soshi. There was no way for them to get a private compartment. They were forced to spend their wedding night sitting up among strangers, and they were exhausted when they finally arrived home. Stopa met them at the station. He had received Grisha's telegram telling him of their imminent arrival.

Natasha was so glad to be in her new home, the home that she loved from the first moment she saw it. The first thing she wanted to do was to sleep. She could hardly stand on her feet. Her eyes burned, her back ached, and her feet hurt. She was too tired to want even to bathe after the long journey. Sleep was all that she wanted.

As they approached the big, white house with its tall pillars, there were carriages parked all around it.

"Grisha, who are all these people?"

"Our friends," he said.

"What are they doing here?"

"They are here to celebrate our wedding."

The house was full of people. The first person Natasha met was Marusia. The two women hugged each other, and Marusia welcomed her new mistress home. It would be impossible to merely greet the guests and then disappear. They had to stay and open all the lovely gifts. And then they had to dance. When Natasha heard the music, she immediately forgot how tired she was.

The sun was rising by the time the final guest left.

"Darling, how are your feet?" Grisha asked Natasha as he held her close to him.

"What feet? I cannot even feel them," she said.

"You go up now. I will be right up to join you," Grisha said. "There is something that I have to talk about with Stopa." He gave her a gentle kiss.

He watched her walk up the steps. Marusia met her at the top of the stairs. She led her into a new room, a room Natasha had never seen before. Natasha began to undress.

"May I help you?" Marusia asked, taking the dress away from Natasha.

"Thank you, Marusia, but I can manage myself. You had better go and get some rest yourself."

As Marusia left, Natasha's tired eyes looked around her. Everything was white—the bed, all the furnishings, even the fireplace. But the drapes were red, and so was the soft velvety upholstery. On the night table, there were long-stemmed red roses. And, on the bed, there was a sheer, soft, red negligee. She picked it up and looked at it. Sitting down first on the edge of the bed, admiring everything around her, Natasha let herself fall on her back. She thought she would close her eyes for just a minute. But she soon fell fast asleep. Grisha found her, still partially dressed, a few hours later. He put her fully on the bed, took off her shoes, covered her, and left the room.

When Natasha finally awakened, it was four o'clock in the afternoon. Upon opening her eyes, Natasha was disoriented and confused. At first, she couldn't remember what had happened or where she was. She ran to the window, opened the curtains, and then she saw Grisha. He was outside, conversing intently with some strangers. Natasha dressed quickly, putting on a navy skirt that fitted around the hips, and a powder blue silk blouse.

Grisha was alone by the time she came downstairs.

"Good morning, Grisha," she said, as she approached him.

Grisha looked disturbed. "Well, well, good evening, golub-chick. Did you have a nice rest?"

"I feel like I have been reborn," Natasha responded, as she kissed him lightly.

"I am glad."

"But what happened? What time is it?"

"It's almost half past four in the afternoon. When I came in this morning, you were so deeply asleep. I didn't want to disturb you. The first thing that you are going to do now, my dear wife, is to eat," he said. "You must be famished."

"No, not really," she said.

"You will be, when you see what Marusia has prepared for us." He put his arm around her shoulder, and escorted her into the dining room.

"Do you realize that we haven't been alone since the day we got married?" Grisha said as they finished their meal.

"I know, my love." She turned to look at him. "I have a favor to ask of you."

"Anything," he said.

"How about spending the night at the old house."

"But it is cold there," he protested.

"But, Grisha, I really would like for us to spend our first night together there."

"Why?" Grisha asked, puzzled.

"I can't really say. I just think I would be more comfortable there."

"I understand," he said, and he really did. Katya's ghost was still very much present in the big house.

"Do you?"

"Yes, and I think that you have a good idea. I will get Marusia to prepare some food for us to take along with us."

They were ready before it got dark. And soon they left the big house with all of its memories. Arriving at the cottage, Grisha started the fire in the old fireplace. Natasha lit some lamps that were placed around the small but cozy rooms. She felt good and secure in this house. The big house was Katya's, and would always be. The small house belonged to Natasha and Grisha alone.

"This is the first time I've had you all to myself," Grisha said. The fire was lit, the door shut, and Natasha was securely in his arms.

"Yes, I know," she said with mock fear.

"Does that scare you?" he said jokingly.

"No, of course not. I wish we could always be alone like this."

After the rooms got warm, Natasha took off her jacket and set the table. Marusia hadn't forgotten a thing. She even included a pair of candles. As the couple ate, the candles illuminated their faces with a soft warm glow. After they were finished, they made themselves comfortable in front of the fireplace and watched the fire throw sparkles out. The crackling of the fire filled the room with enchantment and witchery.

It was beginning to get windy outside. Grisha was afraid that there would be a storm. He went outside and brought in plenty of wood, in case it rained. The wind blew harder. It picked up loose objects and smashed them against the side of the small house. The shutters slammed open and shut.

As Natasha stood in the middle of the room, watching the candles flicker from the draft, Grisha came over and took her into his arms.

"I wanted a quiet romantic night, and, instead, we get a storm," he complained.

"I don't need romantic nights, as long as you are close to me," she said, rearranging her wind-blown hair.

"It is hard to believe that we are finally alone, and that you are all mine. What a lucky man I am! I don't know what I have done to deserve all this happiness." He pressed her tightly to him. Holding her, he said, "I love you more than anything in this world. Promise me that you will never leave me."

"Unless you get tired of me, I never will," Natasha said.

"That will never happen, my love. Never."

The house was warm and comfortable now, though the wind was getting stronger by the minute. At times, it seemed as if the whole roof would blow away. Yet, because of Grisha's presence, Natasha was not afraid.

She went into the bedroom and changed into the red negligee. The twinkle of the light that came through the door was all she needed. Then Grisha walked in with a lantern in his hand. The light lit up the room where his wife stood in the red negligee that he had given her. Her hair was flung loosely about her shoulders.

"How do you like the way I look," she asked.

Grisha did not answer. He simply took her up into his arms and carried her to the bed that his parents had once shared. Natasha made love freely now. She opened up her heart and her body to the man that she loved. The silly passions of a young girl had been transformed into the sensuous desires of a full-grown woman.

For Grisha, it was like being with Katya all over agin. Like being with Katya. Grisha felt like screaming it, as their impassioned embrace strained, and spiralled upward, completely obliterating the hurricane that was raging outside.

Natasha woke up the next morning in his arms. The light streaming through the battered-down shutters told her that the storm had passed. The little cross on Grisha's chest moved with every breath that he took. Natasha felt proud to be his woman.

Natasha wanted to surprise Grisha with a warm fire and the smell of breakfast cooking. Before she could get out of bed, however, Grisha woke up.

"And where do you think that you are going?" he said, pulling her back to the bed.

"I wanted to start the fire."

"The fire can wait. Come here and say good morning to your husband."

"Good morning, dear husband," she said teasingly.

"How are you this morning, my dear wife?"

"I am absolutely, positively happy, my dear husband."

"You stay in bed while I make the fire."

"You are spoiling me," she said, but did not refuse.

After they had breakfast, they went down to the water. Grisha watched Natasha jumping from rock to rock, trying to keep dry. The wind blew through her hair, as she sat among the rocks and sang an old Russian love song.

They spent five days alone together before they returned to Katya's big, white house. Grisha had some surprises for Natasha. He had added a big, wonderful studio for her, which carpenters had worked on day and night in order to finish before the wedding.

Soon things settled down to a stable routine. Grisha was quite busy, but when he was free, he would spend every moment with Natasha. Yet everything about the house reminded them of Katya. And sometimes this caused some embarrassing moments between them. Natasha was confident that, with time, everything would be fine. She didn't let moments like these spoil her happy ones.

Then winter came. Everything was covered with snow and there wasn't much to do. Natasha kept busy by going to the nearby villages. She helped there with the sick. Sometimes she would return at night completely exhausted. Grisha didn't like this and tried to keep her home as much as possible. But she was determined to help the poor, and not even Grisha could stop her from taking food and old clothes to the peasants. They had become dependent on her.

Everything was going well. They were happy, and they had a son a year and a half later. They called him Fedya. He was a lovely child. Grisha was the happiest man around.

The following winter Natasha's parents stayed with them for a while, making the winter days pass quickly. It was a happy home, filled with much laughter and love. Grisha was proud of his son and the grandparents were overjoyed with their only grandson.

With the Spring Offense of 1914, the strikes and riots increased throughout the Russian homeland. Every day there was news of more casualities, in the cities and on the front. The soldiers froze to death in the trenches; and, in the big cities, the factory workers were clobbered to death by the Cossacks. Natasha helped to make bandages for the wounded soldiers. She had seen so much blood now that the sight of it no longer disturbed her.

But that was not all that came with the spring. There was also the new, fresh, soft grass and the budding of the trees. Soon the snow was gone and replaced by the warm days of summer.

Talk of revolution increased. The industrial workers were tired of laboring seventy hours a week for starvation wages. They could not pay their rents nor feed their children. There was even talk of overthrowing the Czar. All this disturbed

Natasha. But Grisha was unphased by it all. He refused to believe that the revolution could ever become a reality. His faith in the present system was too strong for him to even conceive of another one.

Natasha prayed every night for the safety of her family. There was talk of sending all the rich to Siberia. Natasha knew that Grisha and herself were on the top of the list. Their own peasants had begun to revolt. Most of them refused to work, and the crops were left to rot in the fields. Only the faithful ones stayed, like Marusia and Stopa. While thousands starved, good fruit rotted on the vine. The family tried to pick as much as they could, but this amounted only to a handful. The family's big wooden barn was burned down by the anarchists, destroying all the wheat that had been harvested. They were lucky that the house itself still stood.

With the new year, however, things quieted down a bit. But the quiet was illusory. There appeared a new newspaper called *Pravda*, which everyone began reading. It was edited by a man named Stalin, whom nobody had ever heard of before.

People of means soon began to run for their lives. Some went to the U.S.A., some to Europe. They sold everything that they could and left the rest behind. Natasha's parents decided to leave, also. They insisted that Grisha should do the same, but Grisha refused to leave everything behind. They were shocked and hurt that Grisha would not put his family ahead of his estate.

They left for Switzerland, where they had relatives. The next few months were spent in constant fear. Hundreds of landowners had already been killed by their peasants in the name of the new Russia. Grisha was warned that his family would be arrested soon, so he told Natasha that she had better join her parents in Europe.

"But what about you?" Natasha asked alarmed.

"I will follow you, as soon as I have sold everything," Grisha said.

"I am not going without you."

"But you must. I don't want anything to happen to you and Fedya."

"I will stay with you," Natasha pleaded. "I don't care how

dangerous it is. If something should happen, then let it happen to all of us."

"No, it is better this way," he said. "If we leave together, they will be suspicious. I have a much better chance of slipping out later if I am alone."

Natasha did not like the idea, but she had no choice. Grisha made arrangements for them to depart at the end of the week. The arrangements took considerable influence and were very expensive.

It was a dark night, as she said good-by to Grisha.

"Take care of yourself and don't write until you hear from me," he made her promise.

"I still don't think that I should go," Natasha pleaded, although she knew it was futile. "If something should happen to you, I would never forgive myself."

"Nothing will happen, as long as I have my good luck charm," he said, pointing to the cross beneath his shirt. "Remember that I love you very much, so take care of yourself and our little son. Until I am with you once more, may God protect you."

V

Natasha's parents lived in a small but comfortable house. They even had a maid, by the name of Claudia. They were glad to have their grandson and daughter finally with them. They tried to make things as cheerful and pleasant for them as possible, under the circumstances.

The situation in Russia deteriorated quickly. The newspapers were filled with stories of bloodshed and mayhem. Natasha worried more and more about Grisha. She still had not heard from him. At times she didn't think she could go on, but the sight of her son reassured her. Fedya was a beautiful child. In spite of being a male, he looked a lot like Natasha. He was bright and seemed much older than his three years. He loved to sit on his grandfather's knee and hear stories about the old Russia. Grandpa became a second father to him.

"Mother, do you know what I am going to be, when I grow up?" he asked her while she painted.

"What are you going to be, my angel?"

"I am going to be a strong man like father and a good artist like you."

She took him into her arms and held him, and then began to cry.

"Why are you crying, mother?" he said, wiping away her tears.

"Because I love you so," she answered.

Natasha often took her son to Berne. They spent the whole day watching the bears and riding around in the carriage. Then they ate dinner in a cafe. Fedya never complained that he was tired.

The time passed slowly; but even so, it was now a whole year since she had left Russia. So far, Natasha had one letter from her beloved Grisha. Then she received a second letter that had been mailed months before. Grisha said that he was fine and that she had to be patient just a little while longer. There was no chance of selling the estate, because people were not willing to risk their money. He inquired about his son and asked if he still remembered his father. "Fedya, take care of your mother for me," he wrote. "Now you are the man in her life, but only for a little while longer, because I will be with you soon," he promised.

Since that letter, several months had passed without any further news. Natasha carried Grisha's last letter with her everywhere. At nights, when she couldn't sleep, she would read the letter over and over. She knew every word by heart, but she followed every letter with her eyes filled with tears. She could see his fingers hold the pen and write every word. Oh, how she missed him.

Natasha's parents were very good to the young mother and child. Grandpa spent all his time with the little fellow, and even bought him a pony. They became good friends and amused each other.

Then came the news. On October 25, 1917, the Baltic sailors, led by Lenin and Trotsky, had seized most of Petrograd. From that day on, things began to change too fast. The papers were covered with headlines every day. Natasha took a job in a hospital in order to keep busy, because she thought that she was going to go out of her mind with worry. As she was changing some bandages one winter's day, she was told that there was someone to see her in the hall. For a short moment, she could not move. Her feet needed support and her legs almost gave way. Thank God, she said to herself. Finally my love has returned. She ran into the hall with her arms open. But there was no Grisha. Only Claudia, white as a ghost. She told Natasha to hurry home because her father was seriously ill. Natasha was numb as she ran through the streets. It was raining and the wind blew the water completely through her clothes. She was too late. Her father was dead. His heart could not withstand the sad news from home.

The days that followed were unbearable for Natasha. Her father had been more than just a father to her, especially now that she was without Grisha. He had been her confidant; she relied on him for support, for advice, and for encouragement. Now she was really alone. Yes, there was mother, but she was neither perceptive nor decisive. She had depended on her husband in all important matters.

As time went by, Maria Ivanovna came out of her shell. She began to spend more and more time with her little grandson, who was now four-and-a-half years old. She taught him how to write his name, and took care of him until Natasha came home at night.

Sometimes, Fedya would innocently ask his grandmother, "Grandmother, why did grandfather go to heaven now? Why didn't he wait until my father came back?"

"Well, he thought it was better this way," Maria Ivanovna said. "You see, when he is up there in heaven, he can see where your father is, and maybe this way he can help him come to you."

"But I thought, grandmother, that God was going to do that for us. Why is he taking so long?"

"There are a lot of people in this world, and they all ask God to do something for them. He is very busy, and sometimes we have to wait a long time for our turn."

"But since grandfather is with him, he will take care of it for us; is that right, grandmother?"

"Yes, child."

Then the news came that the Czar and his whole family had been murdered. The Reds had taken over and there was a new government. The thousand-year-old Russian monarchy was about to disappear into history. And still no word from Grisha. Natasha couldn't stand it any longer. She had already waited for two years. How much longer was she supposed to wait? Natasha tried not to think about it. He is well. He has to be. She reassured herself over and over again.

One night, as she was saying good night to Fedya, she told him that she was going back to Russia to look for his father.

"But mother, then I will be all alone," the child cried.

"No, you won't. You still have grandmother. She needs you very much. I won't be long. I must find out what has happened to daddy."

She told her mother about her decision.

"If you think it would make you more peaceful, then you

have my blessing," Maria Ivanovna said. "You don't have to worry about Fedushka. I will take good care of him."

Before Natasha left, she went to visit her father's grave once more. She bought some flowers and went to the cemetery.

"Father, what should I do?" she asked him. "Please tell me that I am doing the right thing. How I wish you were here with us. You would tell me just what to do. Good-by, father. I will be back soon." She put the flowers into the vase that stood in front of the well-tended grave.

As Natasha was leaving, Fedya handed her his most recent photograph.

"Let father see how big I am," the child said.

"He will be very happy to get it," said Natasha.

"Mother, if you don't come back soon, I will have to go and look for you and father."

"I will be back soon. I promise."

Natasha entered Russia under an assumed name. She didn't want to take any unnecessary chances. She had only one suitcase and the clothes on her back. She hardly recognized Soshi. There were strange people all about, and it was hard to find anyone she knew. She tried to remain inconspicuous. She rented a small room close by the station.

The next day, she walked to Grisha's estate. The house was in disrepair. The windows were broken and covered with boards, and the doors were nailed shut. The house was surrounded by weeds as tall as a man, which threatened to engulf the house itself. The house, which had once been so alive, now stood before her dead.

There was no one in sight. She went around to the servants' quarters and found an open door. No one was there, either. She sat down on the stairs, where Marusia always used to sit, and stared aimlessly ahead. What am I going to do? Where can I find him, she asked herself. Natasha had been so certain that she would find him here. Then she remembered the old house. She ran almost all the way. Everything was run-down and nailed up there also. She lost hope again. Then, she saw the main door open.

"Natasha," said Stopa, "where have you come from?" He looked around to see if there was anyone watching them.

"Stopa, how glad I am to see you."

"Come in from the hot sun. You look as if you are about to faint," he said.

She sat down and drank a glass of water.

"Where is Grisha?" she asked, when her breath returned.

"I don't know, my dear child."

"What do you mean, you don't know?"

"The last thing that I heard was they had taken him to Odessa."

"When was that?" she asked hesitantly.

"A little over a year ago."

"How come he waited so long to leave? He promised he would come as fast as he possibly could." She began to cry.

"He tried. I can't tell you how much he tried. But it was just hell here. Natasha, when was the last time you ate?" he asked.

"I don't know. But I am not hungry," she said impatiently.

"You must eat something," he said. She did not refuse.

Stopa didn't have much. He made her some tea and gave her some bread and pieces of pork. She ate everything he put before her.

"I feel much better, thank you. I think I had better start on my way now."

"Where are you going?" he asked, concerned about her welfare.

"To Odessa, to find Grisha."

"Why don't you rest now, and tonight I will take you back to town. The trains don't run regularly now. Everything is such a mess. Did you see what has happened to our town?"

"Yes, I hardly knew it."

Natasha couldn't sleep until she heard everything that Stopa had to say about Grisha and about the rest of the relatives. Before it got dark, Stopa took her to the main house. She wanted to see it once more. Stopa was able to open one of the doors. The living room was still intact, though covered with dust. Katya's portrait still hung above the fireplace. Natasha stared at the portrait. My dear Katya, she thought, you should be glad that you don't have to see all this. You were saved all this pain. And Natasha prayed to her as she would to a holy icon: "Please, help me to find him."

The next day, she was lucky to get on the train, which was packed. All the seats were taken, and people were standing in the aisles. Upon arriving in Odessa, Natasha went to look for a room. It was getting dark. The air was stuffy, and the summer breeze was warm and uncomfortable. She was forced to go to the headquarters of the local soviet in order to make arrangements for a room.

"There is one room at 33 Slowjanskaja Street. You go there. It was still vacant this morning. If it is empty, then you are in luck, Miss Natalia Vasilovna Starovotof," said the man in charge.

Most of the streets were crowded, and there were barricades all over. Once in a while, there was the sound of gun shots. Hungry people in rags flowed down the streets like a tired sea. Is this the new Russia? Natasha wondered.

It was almost dark by the time she reached Slowjanskaja Street. Number 33 was a three-story red building, with long narrow windows. The room was still empty, according to the sickly woman who was the superintendent. She led Natasha up to the room. The room was on the third floor. It was the north corner room, with one window on each side of each corner. It was a small room and empty. There was no bed, no furniture — only a big, tall stove.

"This is the best room in the whole city," the woman said, after seeing the disappointment on Natasha's face. "You should be glad you got this one."

"Oh, but I am. Thank you," Natasha said. "But where do I sleep?"

"If you want some straw to sleep on, you can get some downstairs," the old woman said curtly. "But that will cost you extra rubles." Her eyes glowed in anticipation of extra money.

After the woman left, Natasha opened the window. It was dark in the room, but the street lamp beneath her window shone brightly. She piled the loose straw she had purchased into the corner and then lay down to sleep. She could endure all this degradation only by assuring herself that it was temporary. Tomorrow she would begin to look for Grisha; and when she found him, everything would be fine again.

Natasha awoke the next morning stiff and hungry. She ate the morsels of bread that Stopa had given her. She descended the stairs and went to the backyard to get some washwater. Somewhat refreshed, she went back to the nice man who had helped her obtain her room.

"Good morning, Natalijon Pavlivowna," he said, as soon as he saw her.

"Good morning, Komisar Michalowich."

"Did you get that room?" he asked.

"Yes, thank you again, Komisar Michalowich. But I have another favor to ask you. I need a job. Do you know where I can get one?"

"Jobs aren't easy to come by now. Why didn't you stay at home where you belong? You would have had it easier. Everybody is looking for jobs. Why did you come here?"

"Because I wanted to live in a city," she said.

"At a time like this? Well, let me see," he said scratching his head. "Who do I know that could help you? Yes, I know. Why don't you go and see Comrade Smirnoff. He is the head of the employment office. Tell him that I sent you. He is a good friend of mine."

When Natasha arrived at the office, she was told that Comrade Smirnoff was not going to be in until the next morning. She would have to come back then. Natasha spent the whole day listening to people and trying to discover where the prisoners were kept.

When she returned to her room, she was exhausted and hungry. She ate some bread and a piece of pork that she had bought from a store earlier in the day. She covered herself with the blanket that her mother had insisted she take with her. She lay there and wondered how her precious son was doing. She took out his picture and kissed it. I will soon be with you, my little angel. And with these thoughts, she fell asleep.

Natasha rose early the next morning and arrived at the employment office before Komisar Smirnoff. She sat down and waited. She was afraid to meet this new man. Everything about the New Russia scared her. Everyone that she saw these days looked hard and strange. What had happened to those sweet, melancholy people that she grew up with, she wondered.

"Good day. You must be Natalia Vasilovna Starovotof. Come with me, and we will see what we can do to help you."

She followed him into the next room. "How do you know my name?" she asked as she sat down opposite him.

"I met Comrade Fedorowich on my way here, and he told me that you would like a job. Is that true?" he asked with a harsh voice.

"Yes."

"Do you think it is that easy?" he said authoritatively.

"I am sure it isn't," she said meekly, with her heart pounding. She wasn't accustomed to this type of man. To her, it seemed as if the whole Russian race had changed. For the first time in her life, she was afraid of another Russian. But she was determined not to show it.

He stared at her for a while. She looked him straight in the eye. He must have been around forty years old, with a rough haggard face. She was wondering why he had been so rude. She had noticed before, when he walked in, how everyone quieted down and moved aside. She came to the conclusion that he just projected a tough exterior and that, inside his strong chest, there beat a tender heart.

"I will do anything, as long as it is work, Comrade. I don't want to go back to my little home town."

"Let me see your passport," he demanded.

Her fingers trembled as she handed him the false passport. He looked at it, then at her. He did not say anything for a long time. Finally, he wrote down an address on a piece of paper and handed it to her.

"Go to this address. It is the Ministry of Agriculture here. I understand they need someone, but I don't know what kind of help they need. You can find out if it is anything that you would be willing to do," he said.

He got up, came around the desk, and stood close to her. He handed her back the passport and took her hand. But he did not let it go. Finally, she had to pull it gently away.

"I hope that we will see each other soon," he said.

"You never know," she said politely. "If that job doesn't work out, I may be back quite soon."

"I don't mean on business. Maybe one day, we might have dinner together, my dear little Comrade."

"Dosvidaniya, Comrade Smirnoff," she said curtly.

Natasha took a big breath of relief when she finally got outside. She went around the corner to the address that he had given her. She was shown into a big room, which was poorly furnished. Behind the desk sat a gray-haired man, between fifty and sixty years old. Natasha wasn't good at guessing ages. As he spoke, she could see that the yellow, uneven teeth inside his broken, scarred face had taken on a dirty smile.

"We need a cleaning woman. Didn't Komisar Smirnoff tell you?"

"He didn't know exactly what kind of opening you had," she said.

"Well, you are not the right person for it." He turned around and went back to his chair behind the desk.

"But Comrade Sergeiowich, I must have that job."

"You don't look like you know how to work," he said.

"Oh, yes, I know how. Please give me a chance." He sat there looking at her, not saying a word.

"OK, you may start tonight. You will work from six in the evening until you have finished cleaning these five rooms. It is up to you how long you work on them. Just be sure that they are clean."

She had no idea how hard a job it was going to be, nor did she care. The important thing was to be in a government office, where she might have the opportunity to learn about the prisoners that were brought to the city every day. Working at night pleased her. That left her free all day to search for her husband. She generally finished her cleaning around one in the morning. Every night she had to scrub the floors of three rooms; the other two, only once a week. After the first few days, she thought that her knees were going to break in half. But, after a few weeks, she got accustomed to the job, and it wasn't that hard on her.

Natasha had learned that most of the prisoners in Odessa

97

were kept in the fortress. She was convinced that Grisha was among them. That, she thought, was the reason that he was unable to write. Every night she went to sleep and woke up with these words on her lips: "I'll find you, my love, and together we will be free."

Comrade Sergeowitch was still there one day when she arrived for work. That was unusual for him; he usually left early.

"Oh, pardon me," she said, as she walked into his office and saw him behind the desk.

"Come in, Natalia. I would like to talk to you. Close the door," he said, as she entered.

She was frightened of this man. She didn't trust him or his smiles. She closed the door, but remained standing by it.

"Why are you so frightened of me, child?"

"I'm not," she said.

"Why, then, are you standing all the way back there?" She moved a little closer holding a dust rag in her hand.

"There is nothing for you to be afraid of, Natalia. I have five daughters all your age. Come and sit down."

She sat down but remained uncomfortable. She waited to hear what he had to say.

"Natalia, can you write?"

"Yes," she replied hesitantly.

"Good, I want you to work for me as my secretary."

"But I don't know if I can. I am not that good."

"You will be, don't worry. I don't like to see you working so hard. You don't have to wash floors. There are plenty of illiterate women who can do that."

"But, I don't really mind."

"You have been doing a good job. I didn't want to give you the job in the first place. The only reason I did was because I knew that eventually I would be able to offer you something better."

"That is very kind of you, Comrade."

"You may go home now," he said. "I have hired someone else to take your place."

"Thank you. Good night. I'll see you tomorrow morning."

She beamed with happiness as she closed the door behind

her. She would not have to scrub floors anymore. She regretted, however, the fact that she no longer had her days free to search for Grisha. On the other hand, this way she would meet more people and hear more about the prisoners.

Comrade Sergeowitch liked Natasha's amiable disposition and sometimes brought her some of his wife's cooking.

"Natalia, why don't you come home with me?" he said one night a few weeks later. "We are going to have a small party for my youngest daughter's birthday."

"I don't think I should," she said.

"Why not? Is there someone waiting for you?"

"No."

"Then you must come. It's all set."

She had no choice but to go. They left together after work. There were about fifteen people there already. The party was very loud. The young men and women had seemingly forgotten that a war was in progress. They sang songs that she had never heard before. Posters of Stalin and Lenin decorated the bare walls. The young men were all wearing uniforms. After a light meal, they danced and sang more songs.

The dancers kicked dust from the cracks in the bare floor. The young men didn't let Natasha rest. She had to dance every dance. She couldn't tell them that she didn't want to dance because she was married and her husband was imprisoned by the Reds. As far as they knew, she was single, pretty, and a good dancer.

She was finally able to break free and catch her breath in a corner. Then the shooting started. She looked out the window, but she couldn't see a thing. At first, she didn't notice the warm fingers on her shoulder. She jumped and turned around.

"I didn't mean to frighten you. My name is Vladimir Bolinsky."

The young man had been admiring her from a distance all evening. She radiated a calm self-assurance, and her speech was free and genuine. He found himself hypnotised by her charm, and could not resist introducing himself.

"Nice to meet you. My name is Natalia Vasilovna Starovotof."

"You are new here," he said, still looking at her, with his

vivacious brown eyes, which were ready to turn the whole world upside down for what he believed was a just cause.

She noticed that he was a handsome man. She found out, as they talked, that he was a lieutenant and a wholehearted believer in the soviet government. He tried to convince her that the violence in the streets was necessary, in order to make a better world. Yes, he believed very strongly in the future of Russia. Natasha wondered, however, whether things could be improved without violence.

"It is too bad that you could not have seen Odessa before the turmoil. It was a very beautiful city. One day it will be even more beautiful," he said.

"It is beautiful even now," she replied.

"Have you been to the park?" he asked.

"No."

"Then maybe one day you will allow me to show it to you."

"Perhaps."

The mandolin began to play a hopack again, and everyone took to the dance floor.

"May I have this dance?" the lieutenant asked.

Natasha readily agreed. It was her favorite dance. He was an excellent dancer. She enjoyed dancing with him and talking. She didn't agree with all his revolutionary ideas, but she admired his enthusiasm and the idealistic spirit of youth.

It was getting late. Vladimir was engrossed in a political argument with another soldier. Natasha decided to sneak out of the room. She ran down the stairs, but before she could reach the ground floor, she heard someone behind her.

"Natalia Vasilovna! Wait!" It was the lieutenant. "Why are you leaving so early?"

"It's not early. It is late," she said. "I am not used to staying up this late."

"Can I walk you home?"

"Why don't you go back and enjoy yourself. I'll be fine by myself."

"It is too dangerous for you to walk by yourself at this hour," he insisted.

"I know how to take care of myself," she said.

"I insist," he said, and that ended the discussion.

It was a moonless night. Occasionally shots rang out. They walked quietly to her cold apartment house. The lieutenant's boots clicked against the cobblestones. They had to avoid several streets that were barricaded. When they reached her door, he lit a cigarette. They stared at each other silently.

"Good night, Vladimir, and thank you for walking me home."

She closed the door before he realized what was happening. She got undressed, said her prayers, and then fell asleep.

As soon as Sergeowitch saw her the next morning, he began scolding her. "How come you disappeared without saying a word?"

"I didn't want to disturb anyone," she said defensively. "Everyone was having such a good time. But I was tired and had to get some sleep before work this morning. I didn't think that anyone was going to miss me."

"I was worried about you," he said.

"I am sorry," she said with sincerity.

"We were worried, that's all."

"Will you thank your wife for me? She is such a good hostess. I can't remember when I have had such a good time. Thank you so much for inviting me."

"You are very welcome, my child," he said. "Now we must get back to work. I must plan this month's land redistribution. Get me the recent list of political prisoners from the strongbox. Here is the key."

Natasha couldn't believe her ears, as she took the key from her boss. Her fingers were trembling. She hadn't realized that she had been so close to the information she had searched for in vain. But, of course, the Ministry of Agriculture would have the lists. They were in charge of land reform. In the new Russia, this meant confiscating the holdings of the rightful landowners and giving it to the peasants that had worked for them.

There were probably two thousand names on the list. She was only able to skim the list, before handing it to him. But, she knew that she would get the key again and examine the list for Grisha's name. This would not be easy, however, because

Sergeowitch always carried his keys in his pocket. But she wouldn't come this close and fail. Sometime, somehow, she would get that key.

One day, a few weeks later, Natasha noticed that Sergeowitch was upset.

"Is there something wrong?" she asked.

"Yes, my child. I have been transferred."

"To where?"

"To Moscow."

"Moscow, but why?"

"Well, they are in need of men like me. The capital is going to be Moscow now, and they are transferring all experienced government officials there."

"That is awful."

"Will you come with me?" he asked.

"No. I would like to stay here, if it is all right with you. It would be too hard for me to start all over in a new place. I'm pretty much at home here now. Besides, I don't like cold weather."

"I understand, and I don't blame you," he said grimly.

"When do you have to leave?" she asked.

"In three days. My family will follow as soon as I can find them quarters."

Natasha knew that she would miss him. He was like an uncle to her. The night he left, he called Natasha into his office and said, "Natalia, here is the key to the strongbox. Give it to Komisar Nalchick tomorrow. I understand he is going to take my place here. Good-by, and take care."

As soon as Sergeowitch left, Natasha unlocked the strongbox. She trembled with fear that somebody might come in. She removed the prisoner lists and began to search for Grisha's name. She read furiously. Soon, there, were only two pages left to read. She went down the rest of the list slowly. She was afraid to come to the end without finding Grisha's name. Then, in the middle of the next page, she saw it: "Grisha Grillow." She sat there for a few minutes, staring at the name. Her tears stained the prisoner list. Grisha is still alive, she whispered to herself. Now I must try to get a message to him.

She could not sleep. She walked the floors all night. She felt utterly alone. It was like being in a foreign land. She thought of her little son and prayed that he was well. She had received two letters from her mother since she had left. Mother had re-assured her that everything was fine. Fedya had written also—

Dear Mommy,
    Grandma taught me to write in Russian. Grandma and I pray for you and papa every night. I am glad that you gave me your picture and papa's. Now, I can remember how you both look. Hurry back home to us. I send you a drawing I did of my horse.

                                          Your son,
                                          Fedya
P.S. I love you very much.

The fall days were getting shorter and winter was coming on. The cold wind whistled between the bare trees and blew the dried-up leaves that hung from limp branches. Natasha's heart ached every time she saw children playing. She wanted so much to be with her own son. At times like this, she regretted that she did not take him along. But whenever she heard shooting, she was glad that Fedya was safe in Europe.

The early part of winter was marked by more riots and violence. Natasha feared for her life when she walked alone. Work was impossible to find. Famine soon was felt from one end of Russia to the other. Supply convoys rarely got through without being plundered by the hungry peasants. Natasha couldn't understand how anybody could kill for politics. The streets were plastered with pictures of Marx and the other revolutionary leaders.

The rain fell like soft silk. It took a long time to spin a puddle. The sounds of gunfire kept Natasha awake, late into the night.

The next morning, groups of men began cleaning the rubble left from the night's street fighting. The main square was crowded with people. Natasha could see wounded men lying in the streets. Some of them had their heads wrapped in bloody bandages. There were not enough ambulances to take away all the wounded. Somebody pulled Natasha's coat.

"Help me, please. I must not die. There is still so much to be done."

She bent down. It was a young officer, with his chest ripped apart by shrapnel. It took her a while, before she realized that it was Vladimir, the young lieutenant she had met at her boss's party. His eyes were caked in blood, so he was unable to recognize her. She knew that there was no hope for him, but she screamed anyway.

"Someone help this man! Help this man!"

Nobody listened. She could tell that he was praying. He prayed to the God that he did not believe in. She picked up his head and put it on her lap. She prayed with him. Then she felt his head fall to the side. She knew that he would never see the new Russia.

"Rest in peace, my friend," she said with tears running down her cheek. She put his head down gently and went to see if she could help the doctor who was attending frantically to those who still had a chance for survival. He found her before she could find him.

"You over there," the doctor shouted. She looked around, wondering if he was talking to her or someone else.

"Yes, you. Come over here and help me with this man."

She had to step over wounded and dead bodies.

"Cut this man's pants open," he told her. She could hardly hear him because of the moans of the wounded.

Natasha went right to work, not even looking up. She completely forgot about her job. Once in a while she would glance at the red-bearded doctor in order to receive new instructions.

"Come over here," the doctor said, "and hold his head up while I bandage it."

She came rushing over, and held the man's head as the doctor's hands skillfully applied the bandages. She felt an odd sense of familiarity as she watched the big strong hands and perfectly shaped fingers. When the wounded men were taken care of, the doctor got up. He was covered with blood and soaked by rainwater. He turned to thank the woman who had helped him so much.

As Natasha rose from her blood-spattered knees, she looked into a pair of warm, familiar eyes.

"Natasha!"

"Alexander!"

They fell into each other's arms. Neither of them knew what to say. They were both overwhelmed by emotion. Alexander told her that he had moved here a few years ago to work at the hospital with his father. Natasha, in turn, explained her situation to him.

"Doctor, are you coming?" someone shouted to Alexander from the truck filled with wounded men.

"I'm coming," he shouted.

"When can I see you?" he asked Natasha.

"I will come to the hospital tonight at seven," she said.

He jumped on the truck, and it sped away to the hospital.

Her hair was wet and she was filthy when she got to work. Nobody said a word about her being late, since she now had a supervisory position. The hours passed slowly. She left at about half past six and walked towards the hospital.

She wore the same green kerchief that she was wearing in the morning. She did not feel very pretty. The rain had stopped about noon, leaving a gloomy sky behind. It became colder by the hour. Soon it would be winter, which was late this year. Alexander was waiting for her at the bottom of the hospital stairs.

"I am so glad," he shouted, while she was still in the distance.

"Me, too," she yelled.

"Did you eat?" he asked, as he held her fingers in his big hand.

"No, not yet," she said. "I came straight from my job."

"Let's go and get something to eat."

They walked arm in arm to a small restaurant. Alexander could not believe that the woman whom he had loved and lost was now sitting beside him. Her worn clothing highlighted her beauty. He had loved her as a young girl, and now he loved her as a woman. Their thoughts and conversation soon turned to Grisha.

"Are you sure that Grisha is still in prison?" he asked.

105

"Where else could he be?" Natasha said.

"If he is in there, I may be able to help you," Alexander said.

"How?" she asked with renewed hope.

"Once a week, I spend a day at the prison. I will try to see if I can find out something."

"Oh, Alexander, you are wonderful," she said.

"I haven't done anything yet. Don't get your hopes up too high. Let me see what can be done."

He walked her home through the fog-covered streets, and they promised to meet again in two days.

Natasha revelled in the fact that she had found an old friend. She felt guilty about asking him for help, however. He was always doing things for her, and she was always hurting him.

As for Alexander, he knew that he had promised to help her if she ever needed help. Now he was just fulfilling that promise. He was motivated, not by a sense of obligation, but by an earnest desire to see Natasha happy. He had to work hard in the hospital, but the work was easy now that Natasha was here. He didn't feel his tired legs or his aching back because all he could think about was Natasha's gentle face so near to him again. He remembered that the night after she had married Grisha, he had taken a scalpel and cut to shreds her portrait. He obliterated the face that he wanted desperately to forget, but was not, in fact, able to—ever.

The next morning, when Alexander awoke, he shaved for the first time in years. Everyone at the hospital was shocked to see him without his reddish-blond beard, which had become his trademark. He joined his father for breakfast.

"Alexander, you are acting very odd," the father said. "You've combed your hair and shaved your beard. And you seem strangely happy."

"Why is it so strange to see someone happy?" Alexander asked.

"Look around you," the father said. "Do you see many happy people?"

"I guess you are right, father. It is strange these days to be happy."

The following day, Alexander went to the prison, but there were so many emergency cases, that he did not have an opportunity to find out about Grisha.

That evening, Natasha prepared dinner for Alexander. She had only two pots, a tea kettle, and four plates. She lit a candle, combed her hair, and put on her best dress. It was a soft, green dress, with a high collar trimmed with a lighter shade of green lace, and the little buttons went all the way down to her waist. Everything was ready. She sat there and waited, but there was no Alexander. I hope he eventually comes, she thought to herself.

Then she heard someone run up the steps. She knew it was him. He was skipping some stairs just to get there faster. She opened the door as he was about to knock.

"Welcome, Dr. Alexander, to my humble abode."

"Good evening, Madame Natalia Vasilovna Starovotof." He kissed her hand, and they both laughed.

"Mmm, it smells good. Let me guess. Is it a duck stewed in wine?"

"Something better—borsht."

"Borsht? Wonderful! I can't wait.

"So this is where you live." He looked around the room. "Where is your bed?"

"I don't have a bed. That is my bed." She pointed to the straw on the floor, that was covered with a blanket.

"You mean to tell me that you have been sleeping on the floor all this time?"

"It isn't that bad, really. One gets used to it quickly."

"How come you didn't ask for a bed?" he said.

"I was lucky just to get the room," she answered.

"We have to do something about that. And this must be Fedushka," he said, picking up a picture frame that stood on the floor next to her bed of straw.

"Yes, that is my little angel."

"He is handsome," said Alexander. "He has your fine nose."

"And Grisha's eyes," said Natasha.

"You must miss him terribly," Alexander said. He saw the misty expression on her face when she looked at the picture.

"Let's eat, before the food gets cold," he said, trying to distract her.

They sat across from each other eating borsht and bread. The candle light danced in Natasha's eyes.

"Natasha, you look lovely tonight," he said. .

"You are very kind to say that. But, I know that I don't look like I used to."

"If anything, you are more beautiful," he said.

It felt good to be complimented, but soon the conversation became more serious. They talked about Grisha, and her face saddened.

"You will find him," Alexander said. "I will help you."

"You are very kind, Alexander, after what I did to you, you should despise me."

"That is not true," Alexander protested. "Your friendship means too much to me to let the past stand in our way."

"Alexander, I like you this way much better. I mean, without your beard," Natasha said, when the sadness had passed.

"You are not the only one. Everybody at the hospital thinks so too. Especially my father."

"How about a cup of peppermint tea for dessert?" she asked.

"I would love some," he said and watched her prepare the tea.

"I am so glad that you could make it tonight," she said. "Me, too."

"When you were late, I thought you would never come."

"But I told you that I would come, and you should know that I never break a promise."

"I know," she said.

"Natasha, don't be upset, but I was not able to find out very much at the prison today. You must be patient for another week."

She got up and cleared the table with a disappointed look on her face. She had expected this, because he did not mention anything when he walked in.

"Natasha, look at what I have got," he said joyfully, trying to change the mood. "I almost forgot about it." He went over to his coat and removed a bottle of wine and some crackers from the inside pocket.

"Where did you get all this?" she asked, surprised.

"Never mind. Just enjoy them."

"But I only have one glass," Natasha said.

"Then we share the one you have. Let us drink to the success of finding your husband."

"How will I ever be able to repay you?"

"There is no need to repay me. Your friendship means everything to me."

"Alexander, is your wife with you?" she asked, not able to hold back the curiosity any longer.

"I have no wife," he said. "I never got married. Why do you think that I have a wife?"

"Someone told me that you married Olga Fredrowna."

"That is not true," he said, "though Olga would have liked it to have been. I tried to fall in love with her in order to forget about you. But it was impossible to actually live with that silly woman.

"Come on, have some more wine and let's forget those days," he said.

"OK," she said as she drank almost half of the glass. For some reason, she was pleased that Alexander never married. "Tell me, Alexander, how come you came to Odessa?"

"There was nothing left for me at home; and besides, two new doctors came. Father wanted me to work with him here, and it was either that or going to the front. So I decided to come here, and this is where I remained. I don't regret it."

"I almost left Odessa a few weeks ago," Natasha said. "Can you imagine, we would never have seen each other."

"I always knew that we would meet again," he said.

The evening passed quickly; and before they knew it, it was midnight.

"Alexander, it is getting late. I think we had better say good-night. You might be needed at the hospital. Does anyone know where you are?"

"No, I didn't want anyone to know. I wanted to have a nice undisturbed evening for once. And it was a wonderful evening."

Alexander kissed her on the cheek and vanished into the dark hallway.

That night, Natasha dreamed about the days back home. She did not even notice the cold.

Alexander's father was waiting up for him when he arrived home.

"Did you have a good time?" he asked, as he saw his son entering the room, humming a song.

"Yes, father, a very good time. But now we ought to get to bed, because we must be up early tomorrow."

"Do I know the woman?"

"Of course not, father. Now, let's go to bed, if you don't mind."

The following week, Alexander again made enquiries at the prison. He told the warden that Grisha owed him money. The warden himself investigated the case and reported back to Alexander.

"I am sorry, Alexander," the warden said, "but that man is no longer with us."

"Do you know where he was sent?"

"No, he was transferred, and I do not know where. Prisoners that leave here, though, are rarely seen again," he said in a whispered voice.

"But you must have some idea," Alexander pressed.

"No, I don't. He could be in one of a hundred prisons."

"Thank you so much for your trouble," Alexander said.

It was late when Alexander returned from the prison. He rushed over to Natasha's. She was already in bed, a bed that had been delivered only a day before, at Alexander's instigation.

Alexander knocked on the door and called Natasha's name. As soon as Natasha heard his voice, she ran to the door and let him in. She was dressed only in a nightgown.

"Alexander, what happened to you? I haven't heard from you in a whole week. I was so worried."

"I am fine, it is just that I didn't want to come back empty-handed. I wanted to have some kind of news the next time I saw you."

"Then you do have . . ." she said, but began violently coughing before she could finish the sentence.

"Natasha, are you ill?" Alexander asked concerned.

"No, don't worry. I have a cold, but I am almost completely recovered."

He looked at her feet, "You had better get off that cold floor. Otherwise you will never get well."

She sat down on the bed and waited to hear the news. He sat beside her. It wasn't until he sat down that he realized how tired he was.

"What's the news? Come on, tell me," she demanded impatiently.

"Grisha is no longer in that prison."

"Where is he, then?" she asked, disappointed.

"That is the problem. The warden didn't know where he was sent."

"What am I going to do now?" she said in a hopeless tone.

"Don't worry," he said, "We will track him down somehow." He felt her forehead with his hand. "You are running a fever," he said. "You had better take care of yourself or you will catch your death of cold. This room is too cold for a sick person."

"I will be fine," Natasha said, but not very convincingly.

"Come on. Into the bed you go," he insisted. She let herself be covered, like a little, helpless child.

"Alexander, I haven't thanked you for the bed. It must have been very difficult for you to get it. I don't deserve all that you have done for me."

"I only wish that I could have gotten it for you sooner," he said.

"Look," she said, pointing to the window. "The first snow."

She got out of bed and ran to the window. Together they watched the snowflakes drift to the ground. Alexander had a flood of memories. He remembered that it was on just such a night as this that Natasha had promised to marry him. But the promise melted away along with the snow.

"Now, young lady, you must get back into bed. You could catch pneumonia," Alexander said, putting his hand on her shoulder. His warm, comforting hand felt good and reassuring. He picked her up and carried her to the bed. "You really should spend the next few days in bed. I will see you tomorrow and bring you something for your cold," he said to her before leaving.

Alexander knocked at Natasha's door the next morning, but he got no answer. A neighbor told him that Natasha had gone to work. He went to her office, but they told him that she had not been there. He returned to the hospital, still having no idea where she was. He wondered if she had gone back to Switzerland without telling him. His mind was in turmoil all day, and he found it difficult to pay attention to his work.

Actually, Natasha had not gone to work that day. Instead, she went to the other side of town to take a look at the prison. It was a beautiful prison. It had once been the palace of a bishop.

She was not able to find out any new information at the prison. As she walked back home, the wind whipped the snow in front of her. Her feet became weaker and it was becoming more and more difficult to move forward. The fact that she had not eaten much the last two days did not help the matter. She could barely move her feet. Sweat oozed out of every pore in her body, and every joint screamed with pain. Breathing became more difficult.

It was dark and late when she got home. She tried to make a fire and warm up some soup, but the wood was wet and wouldn't burn. She blew on the stove, trying to get the fire started, but it just smoked. She began to shiver; then she was hot. The pain began to twist her body. She put a wet towel on her head and got into bed.

She was not able to fall asleep. She knew that she was very ill and had to get help. She hated herself for being ill. Grisha needed her so much now. She decided to see Alexander. It took her a long time to get out of bed. Her head was splitting. She tried to put on her coat, but all of a sudden, everything went dark in front of her, and she collapsed onto the cold, hard floor.

Later that evening Alexander knocked on the door. There was no answer. The door was open, and so he walked in.

"Natasha, are you here?" he whispered, in order not to scare her if she was sleeping. He went over to the bed, but there was no one in it. Then, taking a step toward the window, he almost stumbled over her. He sank to his knees.

"Natasha, are you all right? Natasha, Natasha?" he pleaded desperately.

He put his hand on her forehead. She was cold now. Then he put his ear to her chest and listened. Thank God, she was still alive. He sighed with relief. But only for a moment. He knew that she had pneumonia. He hurriedly wrapped her in a blanket and carried her outside. It was hard for him to be a doctor now. Never before was he so panicked by a sick person. He tried to control his frightened feelings, but he was too involved.

The snow was heavier now. He ran for a while with her body pressed close to him. He thanked God that he was a big man and strong enough to carry her. He looked for a carriage; but, surprisingly, the streets were empty. He knew that Natasha would die if she did not get to the hospital quickly.

"Please, dear God, don't let her die. Please, God, save her," Alexander prayed. Then, from the distance, he could hear some rattling; and soon a carriage appeared. The back of it was packed with a heavy load. The soldier driving it looked young and cold.

"You there, stop," Alexander shouted. "Can you give us a ride to the hospital?"

"But I am not going that way."

"Then take me as far as you can."

"I don't think I should. I am not allowed to pick up civilians."

"This is an emergency. I am a doctor, and I have to take this woman to the hospital immediately. If we do not hurry, she will die," he pleaded.

After a moment of thought, the young soldier said, "OK, I'll take you as far as I can."

Alexander sat down next to the skinny soldier. Holding Natasha in his arms, Alexander tried to make the young man go faster.

"But I can't. It is a heavy load, and the horses are tired."

Alexander crouched low with his precious burden. He didn't want to get the poor boy in trouble.

"Have you, by any chance, heard of a man named Grisha

Grillow?" Alexander asked not really expecting an answer.

At first the soldier did not reply, and Alexander thought that he probably had not heard the question.

"The name sure sounds familiar," the soldier finally said. "Let me think about it. Why are you looking for this man?"

"I am just helping someone to find her husband." Alexander uncovered Natasha's face. He wanted to make sure that she was still breathing. The young soldier bent over to see who it was that was wrapped in the blanket. As soon as he saw her face, he shouted.

"Natasha!"

"Do you know her?"

"Yes. We used to live near each other. No wonder the name sounded familiar. You are looking for Natasha's husband."

"Yes, but don't tell anyone of this," Alexander cautioned.

"Where can I find you, in case I hear anything about her husband?"

"At the hospital. Just ask for Dr. Alexander Arkadeowitch.

"By the way," said the tall skinny soldier, "my name is Petja Sokolow."

"Thank you once more, Petja," said Alexander, as he was dropped off right in front of the hospital's entrance. It was only later that Alexander was able to connect Petja with the big-eared boy whom Natasha had often reminisced about.

Alexander carried her into his room and put her down gently on his bed. He covered her with several blankets and sat by her bed all night. Once in a while, he would doze off for a few moments; but her slightest movement would awaken him. "Dear God, don't take her away from me now. Dear God, I need her so. Please don't take her away from me." Alexander prayed all night.

By morning Natasha's fever had receded. Alexander felt that it would be safe to leave her alone for a while. She woke up as he was washing his face. She felt tired and drenched, but some color had returned to her cheeks. "Where am I?" she wondered. She tried to sit up, but was too weak to raise her head. She flopped back onto the pillow. She looked around the room. It was a nice friendly room, with pictures on the wall.

One of the pictures seemed particularly familiar to her. It

took her a while before she realized that it was Alexander's parents. Now she knew where she was.

"But, how did I get here? She looked at herself. She was wearing a pretty blue nightgown, but she didn't remember putting it on. She blushed, thinking of the possibility of Alexander's undressing her. She could see her clothes and her string of pearls hanging by the closet. She soon dozed off again. Then she heard a noise, a soft voice, saying something to her. She wasn't sure if she were dreaming or if she were awake.

"Please open your eyes, my love. Please, God, help me to get her well again." Now she knew that she wasn't dreaming. It was Alexander, touching her forehead and stroking her hair away from her face and neck. She opened her eyes and looked at him.

"What happened?"

"You are a very sick girl," he told her. "You have pneumonia, but you are out of danger now, thank God."

"But how did I get here?"

"I found you on the floor, delirious and burning with fever. So, I carried you here as fast as I could."

"It seems that you are always there when I need you," she said in a faint voice. She looked down at her frilly nightgown. "And who do I thank for this?"

"Partly me and partly my mother. That was one of the things that was still saved. Now, you must get something into your empty stomach. I will be right back. Don't get up."

"I won't," she promised.

He came back quickly with some tea and white bread that had butter and jam on it. "I must leave you now, but I'll check back periodically. You must eat and rest." She fell asleep soon after he left.

He was busy that day, as usual; but he managed to come in once in a while to see how she was doing. At noon, he brought her some broth and some kompot. His father, however, noticed how often he was going to his room and demanded an explanation. Alexander was forced to explain, and together they went back to the room. Alexander introduced them.

"I am very glad that we finally met," the father said, taking her hand into his. "I only wish that it could have been under happier circumstances."

"I share your wish," she said.

"How are you feeling now?" asked the elder Arkadeowitch, who stood a head shorter than Alexander.

"Much better, thanks to your son."

"You are in good hands. He is one of the best doctors here; but he won't be the best, as long as his old man is still around," he said jokingly. The three of them joined in the laughter.

That night, while they were eating dinner together, Alexander told Natasha about the fires that had spread through the city that afternoon. It seemed that the entire block where Natasha's apartment house stood had gone up in flames. Natasha's room was now a burnt pile of rubble, and all her possessions had either been destroyed or stolen.

Natasha started to cry when she heard the news.

"It's all right, Natasha," Alexander tried to reassure her. "You'll be able to buy more clothes and suitcases."

"It's not that," Natasha finally said through her tears. "It's just that I've lost Grisha's letters and Fedya's picture. I will never be able to replace them." But then she paused and said, "I guess I am lucky after all. If you had not found me when you did, I might not be alive now."

In reality, this thought provided her little compensation, however. It seemed as though everything were against her. She felt more depressed now than ever before in her life.

As the days passed, Natasha's health improved. She was allowed to get up and walk around the room. She spent most of her time sitting by the window and watching the people outside. Now the house tops were covered with snow, and icicles dripped from the window sills. People covered themselves with furs and looked like bears rushing about. The political situation had stabilized somewhat.

"You know, I have been doing a lot of thinking," Natasha said to Alexander one day.

"What about?" he asked.

"That I should really start looking for a room of my own, until I decide what to do next."

116

He wanted to say something, but she didn't let him.

"Please let me finish. You have done a lot for me. I will never be able to repay you; and besides, you must have your bed back. You can't go on sleeping on that couch. You need your rest, too."

"You had better stop that kind of talk," he said firmly. "You are not going anyplace, because you are still a sick woman."

"But I feel strong, and I have wasted too much precious time already. I really must start thinking about what I should do."

"Well, you can do your thinking right here, just as well. Meanwhile, I will try to find out where they sent Grisha."

In fact, he already had some news. But it was not the best news, and so he decided to wait until her condition improved before telling her.

By the next week, she was considerably improved and gained some of her weight back. Again, she insisted on leaving.

"Alexander, do you think that I could get dressed? It's been so long since I wore a dress."

"Of course," he told her. He gave her one of his mother's old dresses. "I hope it will fit you. She was a little bigger than you. I will be back in a little while."

When he came back a short time later, she was dressed in a brown jumper with a yellow blouse that was a little too large around the waist.

"You look simply marvelous, Mrs. Grillow," he said, with a pleasing smile on his lips.

"Well, thank you, Doctor Arkadeowitch," she said. At the same time, she gave a mock curtsy.

Alexander walked over to the window and looked out, while Natasha prepared tea on the little stove. He had been so busy lately, that he had no time even to go outside. He noticed now that winter had fully arrived in Odessa. With his hands in the pockets of his white coat, he stood nervously. He knew that he was obligated to tell the truth about Grisha; but, at the same time, he could not bring himself to do it.

"Alexander, how about a cup of tea?"

"Fine," he said, awakening from his thoughts—the thoughts that would soon drive her away from him.

"Alexander, is there something wrong?" she said anxiously.

"Yes, Natasha," he said, as he sat down and picked up his cup of tea.

"What is it? Is it something about Grisha?"

He still did not answer.

"What has happened to him? Where is he? Tell me! Tell me!" she shouted desperately.

"He is in Siberia."

"In Siberia?" she asked in disbelief.

"Yes, he was sent there to work in the salt mines."

"But why Grisha?"

"He was arrested as a counterrevolutionary."

She sat there, at first not knowing what to think. Then, finally, with a weak voice, she asked Alexander where he had gotten the information.

"Petja Sokolow found out for me."

"Petja! Is he here?"

"Yes, I met him the night I brought you here. He was the one who gave me the ride."

"How did he find out?"

"Petja is a soldier now, and a friend of his was in charge of the prisoners. His friend informed him that Grisha had been sent to salt mine No. 52 about a year ago."

Alexander left her to her tears. But the tears did not last long. She firmly decided that she would go to Siberia to find her husband.

"But that is foolish," Alexander said. "What are you going to do when you get there?"

"I will try to find some way to free him," Natasha said with determination. "He will not be forgotten like the others. I will not let that happen to him."

"I am sure that Grisha would not want you to do that," Alexander said. "You'll just be endangering your own life."

"I don't care what happens to me now," she said solemnly.

"But you must care. You have a son who needs you. What is he going to do if he loses you, too?"

"He is in good hands," she said, but wished that he had not mentioned Fedya.

He looked at her gravely and ran his long slim fingers

through her hair, as if to strengthen his own resolve.

"Natasha, I am going with you," he finally said.

"You mustn't," she protested.

"Alone, you will be lost. With me, there is a chance."

"I cannot let you do that," she said. "I cannot let you jeopardize your life on account of me."

"Now listen. I know someone that has a lot of influence. He will be able to help us."

"Maybe he can help me, but I don't want you to get involved. You are needed here too much."

"But I am needed there more."

Natasha was quiet for a while and mulled over in her mind what he had said.

"A friend has no right to ask so much," she finally said. "You already have done too much."

"But, Natasha, there is no such thing as 'too much' where friends are concerned.

"I am not going to let you do it," she insisted.

"This is not the first time that I have thought about going there," he said. "You see, I will be able to go to Siberia as a volunteer doctor for a two-year assignment. Doctors are badly needed there, and this will give us a chance to find Grisha."

"And how are we going to make sure that we get to camp No. 52?"

That is not the problem. The problem is how I can take you along. But don't worry, I'll think of something."

After a few days, Alexander had made all the necessary arrangements. He had even gotten papers which allowed him to take Natasha along as his nurse.

There was a moment of silence after he told her. She couldn't believe it. Her mind moved as slowly as the snow that fell so lightly outside.

"Does your father know about this?" Natasha finally asked.

"Yes."

"How did he take it?"

"Very well. He said that I'm old enough to know what I want to do with my life."

"I still don't think that it is a good idea," Natasha said.

"If it means that I can be with you, then it is a good idea."

"But you know that there could never be anything between us, ever," she said.

"I know that. Being near you is enough for me."

Before she knew what was happening, he had kissed her on the cheek.

"You know that I love Grisha very much," she said. "And he is the only man I will ever love."

"I know that," Alexander said, "but that still does not stop me from loving you."

"Agreed," she said. "Now, since we understand each other, when do I begin to work?"

"Tomorrow morning."

"Good, I can't wait."

That night in bed, she tried to picture what the coming months would be like. And she tried to picture Grisha's face. It took a long time to get it into focus.

The small room, which Natasha shared with another young nurse, was comfortable and warm. Since they both were so busy, they almost never saw each other. She worked hard in the weeks prior to her departure. Everyone was pleased with her performance on the job, especially the wounded men who had been shipped back from the front. The sight of the young men, some of them missing legs or hands and others with their guts turned out, greatly disturbed her; but she never let the men see it. They just lay there. And it was hard to tell the difference between the live ones and the dead ones.

The newspapers that she occasionally read were filled with propaganda put out by the new government. Russia had a new face, and it wasn't a very pleasant one. She tried not to think about politics. But had it not been for politics, she would still be with Grisha.

The time came closer for their departure. She bought some fabric and traded some food for a warm sweater. She wrote to her mother once more just in case the other letters never got through. She hoped that mother and Fedushka would understand her decision. The tears that fell on the paper erased the words faster than she could write them. The day before they left, each received three uniforms. She packed her few belongings neatly into a suitcase that Alexander gave her. That night, as they waited for Alexander to join them in a simple meal, Dr. Arkadeowitch presented Natasha with a warm, fur-lined coat.

"It isn't new, but it will keep you warm, my child." And then he took some more things out of the closet and gave them to her.

"I could never part with them before," he told her, "but giving them to you is somehow different."

Natasha put her arms around him and kissed his mustached face.

"I surely hate to see you go. You have brightened my life, just as much as you have Alexander's. He is a different person since he met you again."

"I will miss you, too," she told him.

"But maybe it is better to get out of the city," the old doctor said wisely. "It is getting worse everyday. I don't know what it all is going to come to. I wish you both a lot of luck, my children, and I hope that you find your husband safe."

VI

The train going to Siberia was a cargo train. More than half of the sixty cars were filled with political prisoners. The others were filled with soldiers and a few free men who hoped to make a living on the far side of the Urals.

Natasha and Alexander were crammed into a corner of one of the cars. It was cold and crowded. Everyone kept to himself. There was fear and strain on the faces of the passengers. Natasha, however, was filled with excitement and hope.

The ride to Moscow was not totally unbearable. There were enough food and blankets to go around. In Moscow they had to change to the trans-Siberian railroad. The train that they switched to had more cars and more political prisoners. The train stopped first at Saransk briefly and then at Ulyanovsk a bit longer. Natasha stayed with the train while Alexander walked to the town market and bought some bread, pork, and dried apples.

Natasha paced back and forth on the platform as she waited for Alexander to return. Everything was hurting her. The sharp, scalding wind blew into her face; and the dark clouds, filled with snow, made everything seem gloomy. She felt sorry for the people on the train. She stared at the hard empty faces. There was a baby that was constantly crying, but its mother never seemed to notice. Natasha tried to make the baby more comfortable, but the mother resented her interfering and told her in the roughest language to mind her own business. After that rebuke, Natasha simply sat still and stared straight ahead. She was glad that she had left her dear Fedya at home. She knew that he was safe there, and well taken care of.

Alexander didn't say much. Most of the time, he sat and read by candlelight. At other times, he would just lie back to silently think. Natasha wondered whether he was resting up now for the work that he knew lay ahead. When he would catch her staring at him, he would smile back.

As the days of traveling turned into weeks, the journey

began to get more arduous, and the stops more frequent. The cold was sometimes intolerable. By the end of the second week, they managed to scrounge up a small stove, which made the train ride a little easier. Every station was crowded with army deserters, who were busily trading their guns for bread and bacon.

Natasha became fascinated by an elderly couple in her car. She wondered how they could be so much in love after all the years that they had spent together. She noticed how they talked to each other and distracted themselves from the misery around them. She could tell that they were happy. Even at their age, they were not afraid to start life anew. The sight of them helped to restore Natasha's faith in humanity.

There were two other people who also captured her attention. One was a young, pretty girl, who held tightly onto her belongings. Her long braids were heavy, and she looked as if she came from a well-to-do family. Natasha could tell that she was very much afraid, and resolved to befriend her before the journey ended.

The other person that she watched was a young blond man. Most of the time, he had a smile on his face. He played a beat-up old guitar which matched his voice. He would sing quietly and play for hours, as he watched the young blond girl who sat opposite him. He was strong and happy. Natasha knew that he would be a survivor.

"Alexander, how do you think I can bring those two together?"

"Who?" Alexander asked in bewilderment.

"That pretty girl over there and that young man on the other side," Natasha said, pointing.

"Why do you want to do that?"

"Because I think that they would like each other but just don't know how to get together."

"They will find a way," Alexander said wisely.

"I guess you are right, but I hope it happens soon. She needs someone like him. She is so frightened. It would be good for both of them," she said thoughtfully.

"Maybe it is better if they stay alone. Sometimes it is easier that way," Alexander said.

"Why do you say that?"

"Love hurts. It hurts to see your loved one suffer. It is much easier, sometimes, just to be alone."

"Are you sorry that you came along?" Natasha asked, worried.

"Of course not," he said adamantly.

"I wanted to go alone. You know that," Natasha said.

"I am glad that I came," he said, looking at her with his reassuring blue eyes.

"Me, too," she whispered.

Alexander was careful not to come too close to her. Everytime that their hands accidently touched, he was tempted to take her into his arms. He longed to be close to her and hold her tired head at night. He had thought that he had loved her before as much as any man could love a woman, but he was amazed to see that his love for her had grown with the time he spent with her. Yes, love hurts, he thought to himself. Especially, when all of it burns inside of you.

The misery of the trip increased every day. It became harder to buy food at the way stations. But the plight of the train travelers was slight, compared to the poor refugees who were forced to travel by foot. They fled the cities with their belongings on their backs or pulled them in small carts. Most of them never arrived at their destinations. They were caught in the fighting between the Red and White armies, or were attacked by bandits, or were torn apart by hungry wolves.

"Natasha, are you OK?" Alexander asked one day when he thought she looked particularly perturbed.

"I'm fine, why do you ask?"

"You look so sad," he said concerned.

"It's nothing, really."

"Are you sure?" he insisted.

"Of course. Don't you worry about me. I don't want you to worry so much about me."

"I have no one else to worry about," he said.

She took his hand and brought it to her lips. She kissed the palms. As his hand slid down, she felt him move closer to her. She turned away and picked up a letter that she had been writing.

One night, as they lay close to each other, trying to keep warm, Natasha became obsessed by an awful thought. She could not keep it to herself.

"Alexander, are you sleeping?"

"No."

"Alexander, what if he isn't in that camp after all? What if they have sent him someplace else?" she said, shaking her head from side to side.

"He is there. Petja's friend saw the list."

"But if he isn't?"

"Don't worry, we will find him wherever he is." Alexander pulled the blanket over her shoulders. "Go to sleep now. Everything will be fine."

But she could not sleep. Instead, she sat up thinking about everything that could go wrong. Then the train stopped, and she wondered why. Someone told her that it was because of the storm. She lay there and listened to the frightful storm, which raged and whistled between the wheels of the cars. She moved a little closer to Alexander. She was glad that he was sleeping beside her.

Her desire to have someone near was heightened by the storm. She so much wanted to be loved. She covered her head and tried to shut out the noise of the storm. She wondered how Alexander could possibly sleep with the storm raging outside. The baby was crying again, and people were whispering. Some of the old women began to pray.

Natasha lay there rigid with fear. She felt Alexander's arm around her, but still kept her eyes closed. Had she opened them, the darkness would have hidden him from view. Then she felt his face closer to hers, but she still didn't move. She desired so much to be loved that, for a short while, she let him kiss and caress her. It felt good — too good. Then she caught herself and moved away.

"My God, what have I done! I have no right. God please forgive me," she cried bitterly.

"Don't cry, my dear."

"But I had no right."

"Yes, you did. You felt lonely, and that feeling gave you the right."

Her conscience and the constant rattling of the train kept her awake a long time.

By the time she finally fell asleep, it was daylight outside. They all thought that they would have to help clean the tracks, but the strong wind blew them clean.

The train was slowly, but surely, moving east again. Alexander had been right. The two young people had come together without any outside interference. Natasha could not believe how the girl's face had changed. She smiled lovingly at the young man who had moved beside her. He would hold her hand and sing, or else they would simply talk together. As the trip progressed and people got to know each other better, they would all join in and sing, while the young man sang sad songs that were in tune with the mournful soul of Mother Russia.

Food was becoming a real problem now. Natasha had only a few pieces of bread and some sunflower seeds left. After a few days of wilderness, they finally came to a small town. The houses were built out of the same gray, shabby boards that they had become accustomed to seeing. Natasha, despite Alexander's protests to the contrary, got off the train and went searching for more food. She asked the young girl to watch her belongings for her.

There was a woman running with raw meat and some warm blintzes. The money that Natasha had brought along was long gone, but she hoped to be able to barter some of her clothing. She saw an old woman holding a rabbit by his hind legs. The old woman came over to Natasha and said, "You can have this rabbit for that kerchief that you are wearing."

"You may have the kerchief, but not just for the rabbit."

"But look at the rabbit," the woman said through her yellow brittle teeth.

"You have to give me something else," insisted Natasha. Through force of circumstance, Natasha had learned to haggle over prices.

"But this is all I have," the woman insisted.

"Then I don't want it.' Natasha started to walk away. The old woman came rushing after her.

"Here, I will give you two of them for your kerchief."

Natasha looked at the old soul. "OK." She took off the kerchief and gave it to the woman. The hag grabbed it and took off without giving Natasha the rabbits.

"Come back!" Natasha shouted as she ran after her.

The old woman tried to hide, but some man from the train caught her.

"Let her go," Natasha shouted. "Just let me have my kerchief back."

"No, she has to be punished," someone yelled.

"Please let her go. She is just as hungry as all of us," pleaded Natasha.

Natasha saw Alexander and begged him to free the old woman. After a lot of commotion, they let the woman go. The old lady fell to her knees and thanked Natasha for saving her from prison.

"Child, please take this. Please! It isn't much, but it will help for a while," she said handing Natasha one of the rabbits.

"I don't want it now," Natasha replied.

"Please, child, take it. I want to show you my gratitude." Natasha looked at Alexander, who stood with a bundle in his hand.

"Take it," he said.

When they returned to their car, the young girl was gone, and so was Natasha's warm coat—the one that she had gotten from Alexander's father.

"You shouldn't have trusted her with our things. You can't trust anyone these days," Alexander said.

"But I don't believe she did it," insisted Natasha.

"Oh, she did it, all right. These times have affected all of us. It makes us do what we never thought we could do."

"I will go and see if I can find her."

Natasha asked the people who remained in the car if they had seen the girl leave. They said that she was here one minute and gone the next. Natasha found all of the couple's belongings still there. The only thing that was missing was the old, beat-up guitar. So they must still be here, Natasha thought. Maybe she just borrowed it. She tried to convince herself of that fact. She probably wanted to get some food; and, not having a coat, she just borrowed mine. But Natasha was wrong, because Alexander came back from his search empty-handed. And in a few minutes, the train began to roll again.

Natasha was heartbroken. The only coat she had left was not really warm enough for the frigid Siberian climate.

With each stop now, the train began to empty. One day, just before they came to the end of their journey, they heard the sound of gunfire. Finally the shooting stopped. Alexander opened the wide door to see what had happened. Natasha followed him. A soldier came rushing toward Alexander.

"Are you Dr. Arkadeowitch?"

"Yes."

"Would you come with me at once. We have a lot of wounded soldiers."

"I will be right with you."

Natasha got the medical supplies, and together they followed the soldier. There were red blood spots on the snow, and the screams of the wounded could be heard all around them.

In a few moments, a whole car was cleared just for the wounded. Alexander tried to save the lives of all that he could. He worked hard with Natasha helping. He was surprised to discover how good a nurse she had become. Only three of the wounded died, which was practically a miracle under the circumstances. It took a few hours more for the prisoners to fix the blown-up track and bury the dead.

It was dark by the time the train resumed its journey. Alexander and Natasha had to spend that night and all the next day attending to the wounded.

The sky was gray with snow as the train pulled into town. To their surprise, the streets were wet and muddy. There were soldiers all over. The town was full of strange people. It was amazing to see so many people so far from civilization. Natasha wondered what they were all doing here.

Natasha watched as the wounded were carried to the field hospital. She watched, also, as the prisoners were taken off the train and marched off at gunpoint. She could see Grisha's face in every shivering poorly dressed prisoner. It hurt her to see the open barbed wire enclosure where they were kept like cattle until they could be assigned to the various camps.

Alexander and Natasha were taken to their room. The

rooms were in a recently constructed barracks. The barracks were divided into a prison and a guardhouse.

"Alexander, do we have the whole room to ourselves? I can't believe it. I have forgotten what it is like to be alone. Do you think I could get some warm water to have a bath?" she asked.

"I think I can manage to get some," he promised her.

Soon he was back with a big bucket full of water. He put it on the stove.

"Here you are, my dear. Soon you will have your warm water."

She looked at him, as if to say, "What would I have done without you?"

"Are you going to take a bath?" she asked, as he was ready to leave the room.

"I have some things that I have to take care of first. If there is some water left when I get back, then I will take one."

Natasha found a round, wooden bath tub in one of the rooms, and asked if she could use it. She couldn't wait to take a warm, sudsy bath. She felt filthy and itchy all over.

After she had washed her hair and taken a bath, she felt like a new person. She even forgot that she was hungry. She lay down on the bed, and it felt as if she were lying on a cloud.

The room was wonderfully warm, despite the fact that the windows were covered with thick ice. Then she was sad again, because it occurred to her that Grisha might no longer be alive. But the sadness passed. She told herself that he just had to be alive. She fell asleep before Alexander returned.

He had gone to the hospital to replace the used up medical supplies. He didn't want to be empty-handed when he reached the camp. They promised him plenty of supplies before he left. He even had a chance to wash himself properly at the hospital. Carrying with him some warm food, he returned to find Natasha already asleep. After seeing how peacefully she was resting, he put everything on the table and went outside, closing the door behind him.

He walked into the big room, where all the soldiers were playing cards. He joined them, with the hope that he would learn something about camp No. 52.

"Yes, I just came back from camp No. 52 a few days ago," said one of the soldiers.

"How far is it?"

"I don't know exactly. I just know that it took us two weeks to get there."

"Two weeks?"

"Yes. It is slow going in the winter. I'd give a month's pay not to have to make that goddamn trip again," the soldier said.

Alexander worried about Natasha. He knew how hard it was going to be on her.

"Come, Comrade, have a glass of vodka and forget your troubles," said one of the other soldiers.

"Why not?" said Alexander as he took the full glass of vodka to his lips and drank it in one gulp.

The quiet soldier let the bottle travel around the table until it was empty. The soldiers sang and shouted as they played cards. Natasha was awakened by the loud voices, which carried into her room. The shouting and stamping of the boots continued. She covered her head, but nothing helped to keep out the noise. And as time went on, it seemed as if the voices got louder.

Where is Alexander, she wondered. She was frightened by the men in the other room. She knew that they were drunk. She covered herself completely and held onto the gray, itchy blanket. Then she heard someone say,

"Why didn't that pretty nurse come out here?"

"Why don't you go and get her, Ivan?" another said.

She heard footsteps, then a hand was on the door handle. She stared at the door, waiting in terror for it to open.

"Good night, Comrades, this doctor needs a nurse." The door opened, and Alexander closed it quickly behind him. Natasha sat up in bed confused and terrified.

"Don't worry, Natasha. It is all right now. Those men need moments like this, in order to keep sane. It is hell out here for them."

"Why did you say that?" she asked with an unsure voice.

"What? You mean about the poor men? Well, don't you feel sorry for them?"

"That's not what I'm talking about."

"Oh, you mean about the doctor needing a nurse."

"Yes."

"I had to say that to protect you. They are drunk. You never know how far they might go."

Natasha didn't say anything in response. She just watched him begin to undress. He didn't look at her, as he concentrated on taking off his boots.

"I hope that you don't mind if I sleep in this room, tonight," he said.

"I guess there is no other place you can go," she said.

He put some blankets on the floor and shut off the lights.

"Good night, Natasha," he whispered.

"Good night."

She lay there, unable to fall asleep. She felt bad, making Alexander lay there on the hard, cold floor. He didn't deserve that. He needed a soft bed just as much as she did. She knew that she could trust him, after being at his side all those past weeks. She knew that she had nothing to worry about.

"Alexander?" she whispered.

"Yes?" he said, half asleep.

"Why don't we share this bed."

"I am fine down here. Thank you."

"The bed is big enough for both of us. Let me do something for you for a change."

"I don't think that it is a good idea," he said.

"Please, Alexander."

"If you insist, but I really don't mind sleeping right here."

As he lay down on the bed next to her, he felt every bone in his body sink into the soft mattress.

"This bed sure feels good. What are you thinking about?" he asked, when it was obvious that she was not asleep.

"About Grisha, and the fact that I will see him again soon. You know, I still can't believe it. It seems, at times, like Grisha never existed. It seems like our life together was just a dream."

"Soon you will be with him, and then you'll know that it isn't a dream."

"I only hope so," she said and turned toward the wall and was quiet.

The stillness soon filled the room. They lay there, letting their minds wander. Suddenly overcome with exhaustion, Natasha began to cry.

"Natasha, you are crying." She didn't answer. He turned to her and she collapsed like a child into his arms.

"Cry as much as you need to. It will make you feel better," he said.

It felt safe to be in his arms. He held her gently. She loved him for being so gentle.

"Just one minute," he said, "I have a nice surprise for you." He got out of bed, lit the candle, and then took something out of his coat pocket that was wrapped in a handkerchief. "Here," he said, "this belongs to you."

When she unwrapped the object, she couldn't believe her eyes. It was her little icon, the one that Grisha had given her as a good luck charm when she left Soshi.

"Where did you get it?" she asked, sitting up in the bed.

"The night I found you unconscious, you had that in your hand."

"But why didn't you give it to me sooner?"

"I was saving it for a moment like this, when you would really need something to bring you hope. And besides, I thought if I carried it for a while, it would help me to help you."

Natasha was thrilled to see the icon again. And suddenly Grisha's face appeared as clear to her as if he were standing there. She could hear him saying, "I give this to you to keep you safe until we are together again."

She looked at Alexander sitting there next to her on the edge of the bed, his eyes warm and shining.

"My dear Alexander, I want you have the icon." Kissing it, she handed it to him.

"But, I can't accept it," he exclaimed.

"It has already brought me near my Grisha," Natasha said. "It can do no more for me. Now I want it to help you."

"I will treasure it as long as I live. Thank you so very much." Before he blew out the candles, he remembered what the soldiers had told him. "We should keep our clothes on, Natasha. They often have raids here at night, and you

132

don't want to be caught outside in just your nightgown."

She got out of bed and put on her clothes. As she climbed back into bed, she embraced Alexander and kissed him warmly on the lips. Before Alexander could do anything or say anything, or even think anything, Natasha apologized for her behavior.

"There I go again, doing things that I should not do."

"There is nothing to be ashamed of, Natasha. It is only normal to feel the way you feel. You are a sensitive woman, a woman with so much love to give. Don't ever be ashamed of those feelings. That's what makes you a special person. That is the reason that I love you the way that I do." I should not have told her that I love her, Alexander thought, as he blew out the candle. It only makes things more difficult for her.

The night passed without any attack. It was the first quiet night in a long time. Alexander and Natasha began walking towards the small church that was in town. As they walked, large fluffy snowflakes drifted down lazily, as if hesitating to settle on the muddy ground. Their heads and shoulders soon were covered with thick layers of snow, which made them look like walking snowmen.

They never made it to the church. All of a sudden, there was shooting all around them, and it got louder and closer. People started screaming, and frightened horses ran through the streets in stampedes. Alexander pulled Natasha behind an old burned out shack. The shooting continued for almost an hour. By the time it finally ended, the town was on fire. Half the town was already in shambles when they arrived, and now, the other half was going up in smoke. People ran about trying to save what they could.

When they came out of hiding, the first thing Natasha noticed was a little boy, who looked exactly like her Fedushka. He was crying and searching for his mother.

"Don't cry, I will help you find her," she told him. She soon discovered that he was looking only for his mother's head.

The next few days were devoted to bandaging up the wounded and burying the dead. Natasha felt completely exhausted from her activities. It hurt her not to be able to help the hundreds that were helpless. Children walked the streets with bewildered expressions on their faces.

Natasha was hungry. She could not remember when she had last eaten. Was it this morning, or was it yesterday? Trying to remember only made her more hungry.

After a few days, the town finally resumed its normal routine. The weather, however, had become even colder. Survival was tenuous, at best. Food and shelter were scarce.

They were glad when the day finally came for them to continue on with their journey. On the day that they left, however, there was a new storm. The gray clouds of spinning snow swept into and between the convoy and back up to the sky. Natasha sat in a sled, covered by a blanket, and tried to keep warm. But this was impossible. She watched the vast open spaces, which were covered with a thick, shimmering snow. The wind blew across the frozen wilderness. To take a breath was very difficult. It actually hurt.

In front of the convoy marched the prisoners. They were chained and frozen together.

At first, the journey was not too bad. But as the days wore on, the going got worse. The air was tense with gray sleet. It tickled and pricked Natasha's face. So did the gray frozen ends of her shawl.

They camped that night at the edge of the forest. The trees blocked the wind, but not the snow. They lit fires to warm themselves and to keep the hungry wolves away. The prisoners were given a piece of bread and a cup of warm water as their daily ration. Then they collapsed into sleep.

More men fell by the wayside every day. They were left behind to await their frozen death. Within moments, they were covered by a blanket of snow. No man knew whether he would be alive the next day.

Sometimes, Natasha would walk beside the sled in order to warm up. Whenever she was sure she could not take another step, she thought of Grisha, and this gave her the strength to face the howling wind. With each step she took, she remembered a past moment that she had spent with her husband. Then Alexander would come by and tell her to get into the sled. This would bring her back to the present.

Natasha could not figure out how the convoy knew where it was going. Everywhere she looked appeared the same. There were no roads, no signs. Just snow and more snow.

Whenever a prisoner would drop, the man who was chained to him would immediately tear off his clothes. The sight of this disgusted Natasha. She could not understand how men could turn into such animals.

But as the days turned into weeks, she began to understand more and more about the need for survival. Now there were no more forests and no more wood with which to make fires at night. The nights that followed were spent in holes, which the prisoners dug. The walls of snow protected them from the cold. The prisoners were like snow mummies. Snow was frozen into their clothing and beards. Natasha could no longer see their empty eyes. They marched into the unknown, seemingly not caring what would happen to them.

The cold never bothered Alexander. Natasha's presence warmed his whole being. There were many times when Natasha would watch Alexander sitting by her side. He would be all covered with snow, and his lips would be blue and blistered. At times like this, a wave of tenderness would overcome her. She was tempted to kiss the hard, cold skin of his lips. She was glad that she was not alone and that it was Alexander that had accompanied her.

VII

As they started to head south, the weather became warmer. It was still snowing, but the wind wasn't as cold or strong. The sun itself seemed brighter. As they approached the mining region, they saw more and more settlements. It became easier to procure food.

After two and a half weeks on the road, they sighted camp No. 52, a large settlement standing at the base of a forest. The camp appeared quiet; nothing moved. The only sign of life was the smoke rising from the chimneys. Natasha's heart beat faster with the knowledge that she was so near Grisha. At the same time, Alexander had greater and greater anxiety.

As they went through the tall gate that was made out of barbed wire, she could not believe that she was finally here. She held Alexander's hand, as if to say, "We have made it, friend." He gave her a warm, though forced, smile, and helped her out of the sled.

By now night had fallen, and around them was darkness. Occasionally, a shimmering light broke through the engulfing darkness. The new prisoners were locked away. Natasha watched and began to cry for no apparent reason.

After consulting with the heads of the convoy, the commandant of the camp came out to greet Alexander and Natasha.

"My name is Nikolai Popowich. You must be the doctor that we have been waiting for."

"Yes, my name is Alexander Arkadeowitch, and this is Miss Natalia Vasilovna Starovotof. She is my nurse."

"I am so glad to know you both," he said, shaking Alexander's hand with real emotion.

Natasha was surprised that he seemed so gentle. She thought that all the Red Army officers were heartless and cold.

"We will talk tomorrow," he said to them. "You had better get out of this damned cold."

A soldier led them to their rooms. The barracks that would

be Natasha's home for the next two years stood directly in front of them, silhouetted by the night sky. The soldier led them into a big room. He lit a lantern. They looked around. There were two small adjoining rooms. One room had a bed, a closet, a chair; the other was empty.

"This is going to be your room, Alexander said, pointing to the furnished one. "And that one is going to be mine. Tomorrow, I will get the things that I need."

Natasha awoke early the next morning. She tried to look out the window, but the glass was frosted over. She could not see a thing. By the time she had dressed and entered the big room, Alexander had already built a fire.

"Good morning. So you beat me to it," she said, as he put some more wood into the stove that stood in the middle of the room.

"And how did you sleep?" he asked.

"Like a dream," she answered. "How about you?"

"The same. I already talked to the commandant. Come, I will show you where we will be working."

He opened a side door of the big room, which led down a long corridor.

"Very practical," Natasha said. "We don't even have to go outside."

Later Natasha put on her flimsy coat, covered her head with a shawl, and went outside to look around the camp on her own.

"You can't go beyond this point," a guard told her. "The prisoners live there. It is better if you stay out of there."

"But how are we supposed to help the sick?"

"They will come to you."

Sometimes Alexander would go to neighboring camps to treat the sick. Natasha would stay behind and take care of the minor injuries that would occur at camp No. 52. The more serious cases had to await Alexander's return. There were times when he didn't return for two or three days in a row. On days like those, Natasha would lie for hours before falling asleep, listening to the howling of the wolves in the distance.

Spring came early that year, and she was glad. She was tired of the cold days, and longed to hear once more the singing of the birds. But, most of all, she looked forward to the day that the men would return. They had been working about twenty kilometers away, building a new prison camp, and would not return until spring.

Warm and pleasant air came with the first days of spring. The masses of snow began to melt. There was still no sign of Grisha, which greatly depressed Natasha. She became so preoccupied that she would completely forget about herself. Alexander even had to remind her to eat.

Whenever she asked the prisoners about Grisha, they inevitably told her that they did not know anybody by that name. She had the feeling, however, that they did not trust her and were holding back information. Alexander made inquiries, also. He asked guards and soldiers, but no one knew a prisoner by that name. These were relatively new guards, however, and so would not be expected to know Grisha. And besides, prisoners were generally identified only by their number, which was given to them when they were arrested. Natasha wanted to go to the commandant and ask him directly, but Alexander talked her out of it.

"What happens if Grisha isn't here? And suppose the commandant starts questioning you. You might get yourself into trouble, and then you will have lost everything."

"If Grisha isn't alive, then I don't care what happens to me," Natasha said.

Several days more passed before they received any information. Alexander was trying to clean an old man's badly cut hand. In an effort to distract the old man from his pain, he got into a conversation with him, and discovered a warm soul beneath the rags and filth.

"How long have you been here?" asked Alexander.

"Three years, and all of it in the mine," he said regretfully.

"Would you, by any chance, know a man by the name of Grisha Grillow?" The old man thought for a while, as the doctor bandaged his injured hand. At first, Alexander thought that he wasn't going to get an answer. When the answer did come, it was sudden and unexpected.

"He was killed, God rest his soul."

Alexander thought that he hadn't heard the old man correctly. Before he asked again, however, he made sure that Natasha wasn't around.

"You must be mistaken."

"No, I'm not," the old man said, "If we are talking about the same man. He was about thirty-five, much shorter than you, Doctor, and he had black hair."

"That does sound like the same man," Alexander conceded.

"He came here a few months after me," continued the old man. "We became good friends."

"Well, how did he die? What happened?" asked Alexander impatiently.

The old man's answer was long and evasive. "See all these barracks? He helped build them. When I got here, there were only six barracks. Yes, he was a man with a good head on his shoulders. It is a shame that he had to die the way he did. He should have been a survivor. He talked all the time about his lovely wife and child."

"But how did he die?"

"One day—I think it was last year—when we were deep in the mine, part of the wall gave way and crushed thirty men. He was one of them. I was just a few feet away from him, and I just got my legs badly hurt."

"Did he die immediately?"

"No, he lived long enough to say a few words to me. But why are you so interested in him?" the old man said cautiously.

"He was my friend."

The old man looked deep into Alexander's eyes. Then he removed from under his shirt a small cross on a golden chain.

"Since you are his friend, maybe you can fulfill his last wish, because I will never be able to do it. He gave me this before he died and told me to try to get it somehow to his wife. But I have lost the address, so I still carry it with me. Would you be so kind as to give it to her and tell her that his last words were 'I love you.'"

When Alexander was finally left alone, he found himself unable to move. He clutched the small cross in his fist and sat down, looking straight ahead. How am I going to tell her, he thought to himself.

He heard Natasha moving about in the other room but

could not face her with the tragic news, not now. He was too upset himself to be any comfort to her. He knew that she would need him to be strong.

He went for a walk and tried to think of a way to break the news to her gently. Gently or not, sooner or later she would have to know. The gray fog drifted about. It was gloomy outside, and the weather complemented his feelings. There had been times when he had hated Grisha, but only sometimes. He only hoped that Grisha had realized what a lucky man he had been to have possessed Natasha's love even for a short while.

Later that night, as they were finishing their supper, Natasha noticed that Alexander was exceptionally quiet. She wondered what was troubling him. The only sound that disturbed the calm night was the singing of the nightingale. When Natasha could stand his quietness no longer, she broke down and asked him what was the matter.

His reply came slowly. He was searching for the right words to tell her.

"You have some news about Grisha?" Natasha interrupted.

"Yes."

"Why are you so sad? That is joyous news. We have found him at last."

"Natasha, Grisha is dead."

Natasha's face turned white and the next thing she knew, she was lying on her bed with Alexander bending over her.

"What happened to me?" she asked.

"You fainted. You will be all right."

Now she remembered his last words and was ready to faint again.

"Are you sure about Grisha?" she demanded.

"Yes."

"How did you find out?"

Alexander told her the whole story. When he was finished, he handed her the gold chain with the small cross. It was only then that she admitted the truth to herself.

"I am truly sorry," he said, trying to calm her.

"I would like to be alone now," she said.

The tears did not come until the door was closed and bolted. All that night, she reviewed the last few years of her life. All of it for nothing. For nothing. He was already dead when I was still in Switzerland. What am I going to do now?

She tried to remember how Grisha's voice sounded, but she could not. Everything about him was so far away. All of a sudden, it seemed as if the years with him had all been a fantasy. As she lay there, she could see him at Katya's side, happy and safe. She wondered if God had contrived the whole thing in order to punish her for falling in love with a married man.

The next morning, she got up and began walking. She did not return the guard's salutation. She just continued walking along the familiar path, looking straight ahead of her. The ground, which just a few weeks ago was covered with layers of snow, now had a thin carpet of green grass. There were still a few patches of snow, but very small ones. Soon the flowers will begin to bloom, she thought. The thought depressed her. She wanted the whole world to be in mourning. She hated nature for being so indifferent. She found a spot that was warmed by the sun. She sat down and stared at the camp below. There, too, everything was going on as usual. Everyone was busy at their respective jobs. Everyone seemed the same; only she was different. Then she remembered Fedya. The little boy had no father now, and his mother was thousands of miles away from him. She began to cry, and the tears continued until no more could come. The sun, by now, was high above her. After a while, she got up and returned to the barracks.

For the next few weeks, Natasha kept mostly to herself. Her head was empty and her body numb. It was like living in a dream. Alexander left her alone. He knew that she would have to deal with Grisha's death all by herself.

Natasha tried to keep busy. She worked from early morning till late at night in the hospital. Sometimes she even went with Alexander to visit the neighboring camps. The little free time that she had was spent working the garden that was directly under their window.

Most of the prisoners kept gardens, too. The commandant was very generous and gave them seeds. This greatly boosted morale, because it gave the prisoners something of their own to care about.

The lilac bush that grew right under Natasha's window put

out beautiful white blossoms that perfumed the evening air. She left the windows open, and the rooms were filled with the sweet aroma.

Gradually she began to adjust to the changed reality. Once more she was able to distinguish between beauty and pain. Not everything beautiful had died with Grisha. She stared at the brilliant moon and felt the warmth of the sun. Once more Natasha found comfort and serenity in nature.

Natasha became more involved in her work at the hospital. She even got the commandant's permission to teach Nina Pawlowna, one of the kitchen help, how to be a nurse. Nina was an intelligent woman from a poor home who became good friends with Natasha.

The two women were a great help to Alexander. Now, it became possible for Natasha to accompany Alexander regularly on his trips to the other camps and to leave Nina to attend to the cuts and bruises at home.

Whenever she could, Natasha would talk to the old man who had been Grisha's last friend. On an impulse, she decided to give the small cross back to the old man. He accepted with tears in his eyes.

One beautiful Sunday afternoon, Alexander joined Natasha for a walk in the forest. This was the first time in a long while that she had allowed him to be alone with her. Hand in hand, they walked deeper into the forest, crackling the dry crisp leaves. Occasionally Natasha glanced up at Alexander with her big eyes, which were once again beginning to show warmth.

Alexander bent down and picked a handful of honeysuckles that grew along the path. He handed them to her. Then he pushed together some dry leaves, which she sat on, leaving enough room for him as well. They lay beneath the tall trees and stared up at the sky, where the sun was crowning the trees with its glow. Alexander picked some more flowers and scattered them about Natasha's head. Alexander was enchanted by every delicate move of Natasha's body. Her childlike freshness never failed to awaken something wonderful inside of him.

She held the flowers closer to her face and sniffed the sweet aroma. She started to get up, but Alexander held her gently down.

"I think we better start back, before it gets dark," she said. Her words made him hold her even tighter.

"Natasha, will you marry me?" he said, holding her face close to him, so that she could see that his eyes were full of love.

"No! No!" she shouted.

"You know how much I love you, Natasha. I know that I will never be able to take Grisha's place, but I will make you happy. Please let me try. Let me take care of you, my darling, my love."

"I can't," she said, trying to free herself from his embrace.

He ran his long fingers through her hair and then, taking her head in his hands, he brought his lips to hers. She did not resist the long and passionate kiss that followed.

"I love you," he whispered. "Please say that you will be mine."

"I can't! Give me more time. Not yet," she screamed, over and over again.

The sun was slowly fading away now, and the evening air became cool and refreshing. They walked back to the camp. Natasha's hair shimmered from the red, setting sun.

Natasha was not able to sleep that night. She sat outside the barracks and watched the full moon shining brightly over the desolate landscape. All that reminded her that another world still existed were her mother's letters about her precious little Fedya. She looked at the stars, which shone brightly against the dark sky. For a moment, she thought that she saw a little star flicker above her. Yes, Fedushka, my child, I will be back with you soon and will never leave you again. Be patient just a little longer. Soon we will be together and we will be happy once more. Please try to forgive me for leaving you alone so long. She cried bitterly. She felt forsaken, and, most of all, confused.

She looked over in the direction where Grisha was buried in a community grave. Oh, how I need you, my love. She tried to feel his presence, but there was nothing. She went back into her dark room. She kneeled by the candle-lit icon and prayed before going to sleep.

The next day, Alexander and Natasha left before sunrise to

visit another camp. They were accompanied by a relief contingent of thirty soldiers. They had to go by horseback. It had been a long time since Natasha had ridden. They rode close to the forest. The leaves were already showing their autumn hues and formed a multicolored patchwork overhead.

As they approached the town, Natasha asked Alexander how long they would be staying there.

"We could leave tomorrow morning, if Komissar Antipowitch had his replacements ready," Alexander answered.

"Is he the one that has the drinking problem," she asked.

"Yes. I hope he has stopped, because his liver can't take another drop. He is destroying himself."

The town consisted of five huts and a recently constructed barracks. That night, Alexander loaded a wagon with supplies, and then went to see Komissar Antipowitch to ask if they could leave in the morning.

"Good evening, Dr. Arkadeowitch," the komissar said, as Alexander entered his quarters.

"Good evening, Komissar Antipowitch. How are you doing?" Alexander asked with a worried look on his face.

"You are late. You promised to be here last week," whined the komissar.

"I know, Komissar Antipowitch. But, I wasn't allowed to leave until now."

Alexander spotted the vodka bottle under the table. "So, you haven't stopped drinking?"

"Without that vodka, Doctor, I think that I would lose my mind."

"But it will kill you. Your liver is being destroyed by liquor."

"I know it. But I am just not strong enough to stop. I wish I could have you transferred here. Then you could keep an eye on me. Do you think that would help?"

"You are the only one that can help yourself," the doctor said. "I am needed at headquarters much more."

"You can stay here with me tonight as my guest," commented the komissar.

"But I can't. I have someone with me."

"So, bring him too."

"It is a woman," Alexander said. He could see the komissar's eyes light up with anticipation.

"A woman?" the komissar asked.

"Yes. She is my nurse."

"Then go and get her at once."

Alexander went outside to find Natasha.

"Are you all done?" she asked when she saw him approaching.

"Komissar Antipowitch wants us to be his guests tonight. He sent me to get you."

"Why me?"

"Because he wants to see a woman."

"I don't think I want to go."

"You have to. He is not a man that you can afford to offend. He is a very powerful man."

She straightened her blouse and her hair and followed Alexander to Antipowitch's quarters. By the time they returned, the komissar had combed his hair and put on his dress uniform.

"Komissar Antipowitch, I'd like to present Natalia Vasilovna Starovotof."

The komissar politely kissed her hand. "Please sit down," he said, pointing to a chair.

Natasha was surprised to see such a young man. He wasn't handsome, but there was something attractive about him. His light brown hair was curly and unmanagable. Yet, despite his youth, his skin had a sickly yellow pallor to it. Natasha felt pity for him.

The komissar was delighted to see such a lovely woman. Her soft rounded bosom filled the white peasant blouse and her smile warmed his cold, sick heart.

Alexander didn't like the lecherous look on Antipowitch's face, but there was nothing he could do about it.

"Natalia Starovotof, how come you haven't accompanied the doctor before?" the komissar asked while they were eating dinner.

"I had to remain behind and take care of the sick."

"And now?"

"There is another woman there now who can handle things for a day or two. The reason that I came along is that I wanted to see if I could get some fabric and some wool. Is there anyplace in this town where I could get something like that?"

"I doubt it. Wool is almost impossible to find nowadays."

"So I came all this way for nothing. What a shame."

"There is an old woman who lives on the edge of town. If anybody here has what you want, she would be the one."

"Let me go there now," Alexander said, "because tomorrow we will have to leave very early."

"I'll go with you," insisted Natasha, not wanting to remain alone with the komissar.

"Why don't you stay here and keep me company. The doctor will be right back. You're not afraid of me, are you?"

As soon as Alexander was gone, the komissar got up and started to pour himself a glass of vodka.

"Oh, no you don't," she said, taking the glass from him."

"Only one glass," he begged.

"You know what the doctor told you."

"One won't hurt," he persisted.

"If you want to live, then you must stop drinking completely."

She pulled the bottle away from him and poured the remaining third of the bottle onto the floor. She hadn't realized what she was doing and now feared the komissar's reaction. But he didn't say anything. He just stood there and stared at the empty bottle in her hand.

"I'm sorry. I don't know what made me do it," Natasha apologized.

"Don't be sorry," he said quietly.

"When I saw you taking that drink, it was as if you were stabbing yourself with a knife. I just couldn't stand to see you do that," she said.

He sat down and, with his eyes fixed upon his trembling hands, said, "You are the first person who has cared enough about me to do that."

She sat down as he spoke. There was nothing she could say. She was amazed that such a sensitive and lonely person had been given such a brutal job.

146

"You don't know how hard it is for me to keep this horrible position. I am a man of music and poetry."

"But how did you get involved with this mess," Natasha said.

"The urge to live. That's what makes me go on. I am a coward. I don't want to die."

He put his head in his hands and cried like a hurt child. It was the first time that Natasha had ever seen a grown man cry. She bent down, stroked his head, and tried to comfort him like a mother.

"Cry, my friend, cry. That always helps."

She felt as if she was holding her own son Fedushka. She held him tight. Then, without a word, he took her face and kissed it.

When he realized what he had done, he let go and said, "Forgive me, Natalia Starovotof. Forgive me. I don't know what came over me."

"That's OK. Don't be sorry. We all feel like this at times."

As they waited for Alexander to return, the komissar was amazed at how relieved he felt. He hadn't felt so much alive in years, and he had Natasha to thank for it.

Natasha was pleased, also, to see him smiling. She remembered how, as a child, she had nursed an injured bird back to health and watched as it flew away. She felt now the same emotions that she had felt then.

"Natasha, why don't you stay here?" the komissar said, suddenly.

"What for?"

"I know that I would get well if you were here by my side."

"But I can't."

"Why not?"

"Because I belong with Dr. Arkadeowitch."

"Is there something between you two?"

"Of course not."

"Well then, there is nothing stopping you from staying here."

"But he needs me," she insisted.

"He has another nurse back there."

"I can't stay here, but I promise to come and see you as often as I can."

"Like every three months. At that rate, I will be finished before you return. There won't be any hope left for me," he whined.

"Don't you talk like that. It is all up to you. Maybe you don't value your life as much as you think you do."

He was shocked to hear her talk to him that way. He knew that he loved this woman. She was everything that he always wanted in a wife.

"Why don't you marry me?" he said impulsively.

"What!" She didn't think she heard him correctly.

At that moment, Alexander came in empty-handed.

"I am sorry, but she didn't have anything," he said. "She was robbed last night. The poor woman was left with only what she was wearing."

The next morning, as they started out, Komissar Antipowitch came to say good-by.

"Natalia, this is for you," he said, handing her a package.

"But I cannot accept it."

"Please do."

"What is it?" she asked.

"Just open it when you get home," the komissar said.

"Thank you so very much. You are very kind."

"Come again soon. And remember what I have asked you."

"How can I forget," she said.

"Good,· then I still have hope."

"Dosvidaniya, Komissar Antipowitch," said Alexander. "Don't forget to take the medicine that I gave you."

The komissar watched them ride off and then returned once again to his sad and lonely room.

When Natasha and Alexander arrived home, she opened the package that was wrapped in old newspapers. Tears filled her eyes as she saw the red piece of fabric.

"You know that man had his eyes on you," Alexander said.

"He did not. You are imagining things," Natasha said.

"Well, what did he mean when he said, 'Remember what I have asked you?'"

"Oh, nothing much, just a little secret that we have between us," Natasha answered teasingly.

The next month brought a typhus epidemic. In spite of Alexander's efforts, scores of men lost their lives. The cold and rainy weather didn't help. Everything was muddy and wet. Alexander ordered one whole barrack to be cleared for the sick. There were no beds, and so the men were forced to sleep on the cold drafty floors. More than half of them died of the fever.

Nina and Natasha worked hand in hand. The two women had grown as close as friends could get.

Alexander worked beyond human endurance. Natasha watched him drag his feet through the mud that came up almost to his cuffs. At night Natasha and Alexander would sit by the little stove and try to dry their wet clothes and shoes. They were usually too tired to talk. The crackle of the fire would fill the silence. Outside there was only the rain. They found the silence soothing; and during it, Alexander would study Natasha religiously.

It was almost the end of October now. The weather was beginning to get colder and even more unpleasant. Soon the snow came again. The prisoners tried unsuccessfully to fill the holes in the walls with old newspapers.

The work did not bother Natasha. She thrived on it. She no longer had any strong regrets about coming back to Russia. She knew that she was helping people who needed help.

Alexander knew that Natasha was working too hard, even though she never once complained. He would watch her bending down on the floor next to the sick and trying to comfort them. Her hair would be pinned up in the back of her neck, which accented her high cheekbones and her big, beautiful eyes. There were even times when he felt that she was beginning to love him. But those moments were really only rare instances.

As winter came on, the epidemic began to recede. Everything was frozen now. Icicles as big as men hung from the barracks' roof. The windows froze and would not defrost until spring.

As the days passed, Natasha began to feel weak. I can't get sick, she told herself. She refused to get sick. When she felt weak, she would stop working, only long enough to wipe the sweat from her forehead, and then would go back to whatever she had been doing. But soon she became too weak even to stand. She put on her old coat and started walking back to her room. The cold air bit right through her thin clothing.

She lay down on her bed. The room was warm, but she still felt cold. She pulled a blanket over herself. Soon she began shaking all over. Alexander came in five minutes later, after Nina had told him about Natasha's condition. He knocked on the door.

"Are you OK?" he asked.

"Yes, I'm fine. I need some rest; that is all."

"May I come in?"

She didn't answer. Alexander entered anyway. The room was exactly like his, except for certain dainty touches which made it clear that a woman lived there. On the table in the corner, there were some evergreens. Above her head by the bed, Alexander noticed a pencil sketch. He couldn't recognize it at first, but as he came closer, he could tell that it was of Grisha. A string of pearls framed the picture, along with a handful of dried honeysuckles.

"Nina told me that you haven't been feeling well."

"She just worries too much," said Natasha.

Her whole body seemed to twist as she shivered.

"You have a fever. You are ill, Natasha. Why didn't you say something sooner?"

"I'll rest in bed until tomorrow. I will be fine in the morning," she insisted.

"No, you will stay in bed until you are well. I don't want you to get pneumonia again. You have the flu, that's all. But you have to take care of yourself. If you don't, complications may set in. Then you will really be sick. Promise me that you will follow my medical advice."

"I promise. But what about those that are really ill," she said, concerned about the patients.

"Nina will help. And, besides, there aren't as many patients now as before. We can handle it. Don't you worry about it.

"You had better get undressed, and put your feet in hot water. Then I'll send Nina in to give you a rubdown."

Before he left her room, he stared once more at the small sketch above her head. It was the first time he ever felt jealous of a dead man. Even dead, he still had a hold over her. Alexander felt hurt, as he left her room.

She slept comfortably that night. She was relieved to find out that she had not contracted typhus. In a few days, she was well enough to return to work.

It was Christmas Eve again. Alexander stood in front of the little Christmas tree that he and Natasha had decorated. He waited for Natasha to come out of her room. As he waited for her to appear, he remembered other Christmas Eves, long ago, that they had spent together. He thought about that one Christmas when Natasha had worn a beautiful white gown, which shimmered from the hundreds of Christmas candles. Now Natasha was wearing a simple red dress that she made from the fabric that she had received from Komissar Antipo-witch. Nevertheless, she never appeared more beautiful to Alexander than she did at this moment.

He stood still as she approached him. Tonight there was something very special about her. She was quiet, and her lips had a faint tender smile. Alexander and Natasha stood listening to the sounds of Christmas carols coming from the prisoners' quarters. The Savior's birth was remembered even in this godforsaken place.

Natasha went over to the door and opened it. Side by side, they stood in the doorway and sang the songs of Christmas. After they ate their Christmas Meal, they sat down in front of the fire and reminisced about the good old days. Natasha recalled the Christmases of her youth, when her father used to load a sled full of presents and deliver them to the poor.

They were laughing for the first time in a long while. The desolation of their surroundings had temporarily vanished. A little later Alexander got up, went to his room, and returned with a package that was tied with a blue ribbon.

"Darling, this is for you," he said and was surprised at himself for addressing her so intimately.

Natasha unwrapped it slowly. It was a lovely green sweater. As she picked it up, a soft silk scarf fell to the floor. Draping it around her neck, she could feel the soft silk rub against her cheeks.

"How wonderful it is. I almost forgot how silk feels," she remarked.

Alexander was delighted to see that her eyes sparkled like a small child who had gotten the Christmas present that he most wanted.

She came over and put her arms around him.

"You are very sweet to me," she said, as she gave him a gentle kiss. She started to go back to her chair, but he restrained her.

"I feel horrible that I have no present for you," Natasha said.

"I don't need a present from you," he replied. "Your presence is enough for me."

"Alexander, do you still want to marry me?" she asked nonchalantly.

He was certain that he had not heard her correctly. "What did you just say?"

"I said, do you still want to marry me?"

He was too stunned to even answer yes. When the word finally did come, it burst forth as a shout, which was loud enough for the prisoners to hear hundreds of yards away.

"Then I accept," she said, simply and softly. "And this time, I mean to go through with it."

"I'm not taking any chances, this time, with a long engagement. Let us be married tomorrow," he said.

Just then there was a knock on the door. Several soldiers were standing there. They told Alexander that they had been involved in a drunken brawl and that one of their comrades had been injured. They asked Alexander if he would come to the barracks and take a look at the injured man. Alexander kissed Natasha and told her that he would be back shortly. Then he left with the soldiers.

He came back several hours later. His clothes were soaked from being out in the falling snow. He removed his shirt and stood by the stove, trying to warm himself.

Natasha heard the door slam when he came in. She had been lying in bed but not sleeping. She came out of her room in a long white linen nightgown, which trailed on the floor behind her.

As she came closer, Alexander held out his arms to her; and she placed her head against his broad, manly chest. She could not longer hold back her womanly instincts. Her mind freed her body to love and be loved.

Alexander's fingers trembled as he unbuttoned her nightgown, which slid to the floor. Now she was no longer a friend or a nurse, but a woman. A woman who responded to her desires and to his. He picked her up and carried her to bed. He stared at her nude body but was afraid to actually touch it, because he feared that he would awaken from a dream. But the dream continued as their bodies touched and merged. And the dream did not end even when the morning light kissed good-by to the night.

Grisha had been a passionate lover, but he was too egotistical to be compassionate. He was only able to skim the surface of Natasha's needs. Alexander's lovemaking had greater force, but it was a force that was nurtured by gentleness and consideration. Grisha was capable of giving pleasure, but Alexander was able to stoke the very fires of Natasha's soul.

When she awoke, she could feel his arms around her. He propped himself up on one pillow and looked at her without saying anything.

"What are you thinking about?" she asked.

"Only that I wish that I could dress you in the finest silks and give you a bed of feathers to lie on. One day you will have these things. I promise."

"Having you is enough. Now and forever," she said. And then they kissed and hugged until it was time to get up.

As Alexander got out of bed, he noticed that Grisha's picture was no longer hanging on the wall. Now there were only the pearls. And a handful of dried honeysuckles.

The first thing that Alexander did that morning was to ask the commandant to perform the wedding ceremony. Nikolai Popowich was not the least surprised about the news.

"I figured that this would happen sooner or later," he said. "I wish you all the happiness in the world. But I don't know if I can marry anyone."

"If you can bury the dead, then you can marry us."

"I don't know if it would be legal."

"It will be legal. It will be legal for us, and that is all that matters to us," Alexander said, as he put his arm around Natasha's shoulders.

"Why don't you wait until you get home. You have less than a year left in your assignment here," the commandant said.

"We don't want to wait that long," Alexander insisted.

Having no other alternative, the commandant proceeded to marry them. That night, even as he held her tight, Alexander still couldn't believe that Natasha was finally his wife.

By the time that spring came, the camp had grown considerably in size. One cold night in March, more than five hundred new prisoners arrived. The prisoners had to remain outside until new barracks could be built. They were lucky that it was getting warm now and that the freezing weather had passed.

The barracks were built relatively quickly, and things soon returned to normal. The men would leave for the mine around dawn and return late at night. They were weak, and most of them looked like old men. Natasha pitied them. She helped them whenever she could, but there wasn't very much that she could do to ease their suffering.

One day Natasha asked the camp commandant if she could start a camp recreation hall and library.

"I don't know why you want to start a library for these men," answered the commandant.

"But they need something to lessen their plight," she insisted.

"Most of them cannot even read."

"I know that. But the ones that can will be able to read to those who can't."

The commandant was still unconvinced. However, Natasha was certain that if she kept working on him, he would eventually relent and grant her request.

"I will teach the ones that cannot read," she proposed.

"When are you going to do that?" he asked.

"On Sundays." That was the one day that she was free.

"OK. Let me see what I can do."

Natasha thanked the commandant profusely and told him that he would not regret his decision.

Soon the books were ordered, and Natasha even got permission from the commandant for the prisoners to build themselves a recreation hall during their free time. Sasha Galenko, the acknowledged leader of the prisoners, liked Natasha's idea.

"Don't worry, we will have the recreation building built as soon as possible," he told her. "And we will build tables and shelves and chairs also."

Every night, after returning from the mine, the men still found energy to work on the recreation building. They cut down trees, laid the foundation, and sang as they worked. They did not mind the work because they were working on something of their own, something for themselves.

In four weeks, the building was finished, including the furniture. Natasha placed some flower pots on the window sills. The men were proud of their work and enjoyed the fruits of their labors.

The books finally arrived, but Natasha was disappointed to see that most of them were propaganda manuals. There was plenty of Marx and Lenin, but no poetry or art. Natasha was disappointed but not discouraged. She put the books in order, hung up the posters of Lenin, and made ready to being her reading classes.

One Saturday, a day before she was to begin teaching, Alexander came to see how she was doing. Natasha was so busy putting the finishing touches on the building that she did not notice him at first.

"How long have you been standing there?" she asked finally.

"Oh, not too long, but long enough to see that you are working yourself to death."

"Well then, why don't you help, instead of standing there, my love?" She handed him a poster of Trotsky.

"How come you are doing all this yourself? I thought that the men were supposed to help."

"I know. But I wanted everything to be finished by tomorrow, and the men are busy all day today working in the mines. Besides, the finishing touches are woman's work. How does it look?" she asked, trying to change the subject of conversation.

"It looks great."

She jumped down from the chair she was standing on and walked right past him to the table, where flowers were standing in glass jars and bottles. He came up behind her and held her around the waist.

"Alexander, not here," she protested.

"What is wrong with here?"

"Someone might see us."

"So what! I want the whole world to see how much I love my wife."

She let him hold her, but only for a moment. Then she went back to work.

"You know, Natasha, there are moments when I am jealous of the prisoners. They get to see you more than I do."

"You don't really mean that," she said.

"I do."

"Then you should be ashamed of yourself," she said with mock annoyance.

Alexander walked around the room. "Don't tell me that the men made all these games." Alexander was surprised to see the magnificent chess sets that the men had carved.

"Yes, the men made them all themselves."

"Darling, I almost forgot. You received a package today from Komissar Antipowitch."

"Not another one!" she said. "I have written him so many times, telling him not to send me anything. And yet, every week something new arrives."

"That man is in love with you," Alexander said.

"No, he isn't. He is just grateful, that's all." In spite of her protests, she appreciated all that the komissar had done for her.

In the months that followed, Natasha was happier than she had ever been before. Whenever she remembered Grisha, she felt slightly guilty about her newfound happiness. But she told herself that he would have wanted her to be happy. She had loved him as much as a woman could, while he was alive, and nothing more could rightfully be asked of her. Thinking about her son, so far away from her, also made her sat at times.

But, Alexander always managed to brighten even these moments.

"Love, we only have a few more months left here," he would tell her. "Please be patient. Soon you will be with Fedushka again, and we will be one happy family."

Sometimes, as she lay by his side at night, Natasha would cry for joy at having such a wonderful man as Alexander. She would pray to God to take care of him, and to help her always to make him happy. With her head on his strong chest, and secure in his arms, she would fall asleep, feeling free to dream of her mother and Fedya.

Fall was on its way. It rained a lot, and the fog was so thick in the mornings it was difficult to see the barracks. The smell of dry leaves and grass once more filled the air. Everything looked gloomy and wet, and it got colder everyday. Soon the trees and bushes stood bare, revealing the fact that all the birds had gone south.

Before winter set in, Alexander saw to it that he had plenty of wood for the hospital. He wanted to make sure that his patients would not freeze, as they did the previous winter.

By the time winter came, Natasha knew that she was pregnant. She didn't want to tell Alexander. He had too many other things to worry about now. As the days wore on, she found herself tiring more and more easily, but she tried not to show it. She always had a warm and loving smile for everyone.

One winter night, as they sat by their black stove, Alexander watched her as she was mending his socks. She looked so lovely, he thought. The warmth of the stove made Natasha's cheeks red, and her eyes sparkled from the light of the candle. But there was a worried look on her face, and Alexander could see it.

"Darling, is there something wrong?" he asked.

"No, not really," she replied.

"But what is it? What makes you so sad? You can tell me."

"You won't like it."

"Tell me, come on darling." He took her face in his hands.

"Alexander, we are going to have a baby."

At first, he was too stunned to say anything. "I am going to be a father?" he asked in disbelief.

157

"Yes, I am sorry."

"Why sorry? Oh, I know. It isn't the way we planned. But everything will be OK."

"Some doctor I am," he said, scratching his head. "I could not even tell that my own wife was pregnant."

"What are we going to do?" she asked.

"We are still going through with our plans. Nothing is going to stop us."

"But what happens if that substitute doctor doesn't arrive in time? What then?"

"He will be here. Don't you worry your little head about it."

"I can't help but worry," she said.

"From now on, you must promise not to work so hard. Do you understand me? I don't want anything to happen to our child."

"I am a strong woman. You have nothing to worry about."

Alexander was a little worried. But he did not let her know it. As much as he wanted a child, Alexander regretted the fact that it was going to be such a burden on Natasha. Her health and safety were most important to him.

The month that followed was knifing cold, with the wind blowing once more through the white-covered fields. Once again, the branches were loaded with heavy snow. The little crystals shimmered in the cold winter sun.

One day, Natasha was walking home from the women's camp. She kept her hands in her coat pockets, but the flimsy material did not warm them a bit. The cold wind that blew into her face made her feel as though she were going to lose her nose and her chin. She was glad when she finally reached her door. It was colder this day than before, and Alexander was not there to warm up the rooms. Since he would be gone for another week, she would have to keep the fire going herself. She took off her coat and lit the stove. Then she ate what she had and went to bed, hoping that she wouldn't be awakened by some kind of emergency. Ever since the new commandant took over, it seemed like there was always some emergency.

Natasha didn't like him. He was a mean and heartless man. He was about fifty-five years old, with a gray face that matched his hair. He pushed the men harder than their bodies could tolerate. Many more died than in the previous year.

Natasha was no longer allowed to give reading lessons to the men on Sundays. The commandant insisted that she wasn't teaching them enough politics. He himself took over the political instruction, but the men stopped coming voluntarily. Therefore, the commandant ordered that attendance at classes was mandatory. If an absentee were discovered, he wouldn't get his food rations for two days. It wasn't the same. The men sat in the classes and listened, but they did not really hear.

Natasha watched the poor men returning to the camp at night. The sight of them dragging their frozen feet behind them sickened her, and she was glad that she soon would be leaving.

As she lay in her bed, she thought about the past few years, and how everything had changed. Then she thought how it was going to be when she had a nice home to live in and her son by her side. The wolves howled and barked this night even louder than the previous nights. The sound upset her. She pulled the covers over her head and tried to fall asleep.

It stormed the day that Alexander returned. It was late when he entered the gate. The new commandant went out to talk to the man that had just entered. He was very friendly to Alexander, at first, because he had asked the doctor to do him a favor.

"Good evening, Dr. Arkadeowitch. Did you get the radio?" he asked.

"No, I'm sorry."

"But why not?"

"The black market prices are higher than you thought," he answered.

"Damn!" the commandant shouted. Then he said, "Did you tell him who it was for?"

"Yes," said Alexander. "You'll get one when he gets the money he wants, and not before then."

"The next time, I will go myself and show him who he is dealing with."

The commandant turned around and walked back to his quarters, slamming the door behind him like a spoiled child.

Alexander ignored the commandant's anger. He was unpacking his medical supplies, when he heard Natasha come up. Seeing her warm and smiling face, he soon forgot his long and tiresome journey.

"How are you, dear?" He had worried about leaving her with the new commandant.

"I am fine. How about you? I didn't think that you would make it back tonight in this horrible weather."

"Did you hear anything about the new dotor?" he asked her.

"Nothing at all. He probably won't travel in this storm. It is terribly dangerous out there."

"You're right. It seems as if this winter is much colder than last year," he said, as they walked up the steps to their warm rooms.

"How is Komissar Antipowitch?" Natasha asked.

"He is fine and doing very well. He sends his deepest regards and asked why you didn't accompany me on this trip."

"What did he say when you told him the reason?"

"Nothing much. I think he was a little hurt. But, the day that I left, he gave me this to give to you, along with his best wishes." He reached into his coat pocket, and took out a squashed little package.

As Natasha opened it, her face broke into a smile.

"Thank you so much, my dear Antipowitch," she exclaimed. "Look, Alexander, a nice warm pair of stockings. Mine are all worn out. How did he know exactly what I needed?"

"I don't know. But it seems as if he always knows."

"Yes, and how did he like what I gave him?"

"He liked them very much. He put them by his bed and said that those dried flowers will warm and sweeten his days. He promised to always keep them by his bedside."

Natasha had wanted to give something to Komissar Antipowitch. He had always been so kind to her. So, she sent him the flowers which she had collected at the end of the summer. They were the only thing that she had to give.

"Here, I brought you something, too," Alexander said to Natasha.

"Really!"

"Here, darling. Sit down," he said, offering her a chair.

She sat down and watched passively as he removed her worn and muddy shoes.

"I have a new pair of warm shoes for you," he said proudly. "I don't know if they are the right size. I have never bought shoes for you before."

They were, in fact, at least two sizes too big.

"I'm sorry," he said dejectedly.

"But, Alexander, when I wrap my feet with a rag, they will be just right."

"And that is not all. Here, I bought you a skirt, too."

Natasha was too overjoyed to even ask how Alexander was able to acquire all these wonderful gifts. She put on her gray skirt and her new shoes and felt like a queen. She clicked her heels, and after making a few circuits around the room, she fell into Alexander's loving arms.

"Thank you for being so good to me," she said.

"I am just sorry that I can't do more for you. But soon, my love, we will be free; and then I will show you how wonderful and beautiful you are."

"You are so good." She almost said 'I love you,' the one thing that Alexander most wanted to hear. But she was not yet ready to say it.

The larks were returning, signifying the coming of spring. The bare trees began to fill with buds once more, and slowly the snow began to slide down the roofs. The smell and feel of mud were everywhere. Still there was no sign of the new doctor.

Natasha was now clearly showing her pregnancy. She insisted on leaving, however, as soon as they heard something about the new doctor.

By now things really got hard at the camp. Many men had tried to escape. Most were shot before they were a mile from camp. Natasha prayed for those who got further. She hoped that they would escape the hunger, the cold, and wild animals. At the women's camp, things were not going well, either. There were more suicides than ever.

Then, one day, the head guard was knifed to death at the women's barracks. The guard was called Bulldog because of his looks and manner. By the time Alexander got there the body was already gone, but there was blood all over the walls and floor. The women that slept in that barracks were taken outside and subjected to a long harangue by the commandant.

"You scum! I'll show you where all this gets you," he shouted at the women who stood in front of him with expressionless faces. "You think you have it bad now. You'll soon find out just how cruel I can get. Do you think that I like to be in this stinking hole, watching you? But you'll learn. I'll teach you. You dirty swine."

He then ordered every woman who slept in the barracks to be shot, one by one, while the others looked on. Alexander was amazed to see how bravely the women accepted their punishment. Not one of them screamed or broke into hysterical whimpers.

Natasha had not witnessed the incident and only later found out about it from Alexander.

"Darling, what happened?"

"The Bulldog is dead."

"I can't say that I am sorry. Who did it?"

"The women."

"The women? But, how?"

"They stabbed him to death, with knifes and forks. You know how terribly he treated them."

"He deserves to be dead, but what will happen to the poor women?"

"It has already happened," Alexander said solemnly.

"What has already happened?" Natasha asked, with fear in her eyes.

"They were all shot." Natasha felt her knees go soft under her and had to sit down.

"Who was involved?" she wanted to know.

Alexander did not want to tell her, but he knew that she would find out eventually.

"All of Barracks No. 2," he finally said.

"All of them?"

"Yes, darling. Even Maria."

Maria was a young, skinny blonde girl, whom Natasha had befriended. Natasha was hoping that, one day, she would be

162

able to help Maria get out. Maria was a fragile girl with a good mind. She had come from a well-to-do home, and she had studied music since she was six years old. Her parents, however, were Jewish; and that was the reason they had sent her here. The rest of her family had been killed by the cossacks.

Natasha went outside and sat on a rock where the garden had been. She cried beneath the warm sun, which showed no sign of caring.

"You shouldn't be shining," she said, looking up at the big ball of bright fire. She put her hands on her rounded tummy, which was hard and tight. She felt the child violently kicking and moving inside her. He sure is a rough one, she thought. Nothing like Fedushka. What are you doing, my dear Fedushka, my precious little boy? Just a little longer and mommy will be with you again. And I will never leave you again. I promise.

She sat there until the sun had begun to set. The red, bright ball reminded her of the dead Bulldog, whose real name was Trebowitch. His head used to get red, like the sun, when he got into one of his rages.

Trebowitch had come at the same time as the new commandant. The two of them were very much alike. Trebowitch was a big man, with a shaved head, and a face and neck which were covered with pimples. These made him look even more ugly. He was never seen without a whip, which he held in his fat hands. His name was richly deserved, and so was his death.

Alexander had good news for Natasha when he saw her later.

"Darling, the new doctor has arrived," he told her.

"Do you really mean it?"

"The messenger was just here and told me that we can leave as soon as we are ready."

"I can't believe it! When do you think we can actually start?"

"As soon as we can get a horse and wagon."

"But where are we going to get them?"

"A man in a little village not far from here promised them to me. I treated his son for typhus."

Preparations for the trip were made with care. Their hearts were full of joy. Yet, at the same time, they hated to leave the poor prisoners behind to rot away from overwork and poor food.

VIII

They left on a bright spring morning several days later. Natasha looked back at the camp, as the horse galloped at full speed along the country road.

The road went by the cemetery. They stopped when they came to it. For the last time, Natasha put some flowers at the foot of Grisha's grave. The wooden cross was badly battered from the strong wind and heavy rain. She knelt down at the grave and said a dosvidaniya to her first love—the man who had awakened womanly passions in her breast and the man who would never see his son fully grown. It all seemed so long ago now, and yet, everything was still so close and so real. Natasha's hands began to tremble, and she could not hold back the tears. Alexander practically had to carry her into the wagon.

Just before sundown, they came to a little birch forest. The leaves of the trees swayed gently in the cool evening breeze. It reminded them of their home, and so they decided to camp there for the night.

The days that followed were more arduous. The towns were fewer, and at times they had to go on hungry and thirsty. On their tenth day of travelling, it began to pour. They were both drenched before Alexander was able to put up the portable tent that was just big enough for the two of them.

"Are you sure that you feel all right?" he asked, as he saw her make a painful face.

"I will be fine, as soon as I lie down."

"Are you sure?" he persisted.

"It is just my back. It feels as if it is going to break.

She lay down and he massaged it for her.

"I told you we should rest more," he said.

"I refuse to hold us back," she said bravely. "I am too anxious to see my son again."

"I still think that it really would be better if we stopped in the next town and waited for the baby to be born," Alexander said.

"No, once we have the child, it will be even harder for us to get out of Russia," Natasha argued.

"That doesn't matter if it is too hard on you as it is."

"I will be fine, just a little rest and then I will be as good as new." She tried to convince herself and her husband.

"I love you, my brave, strong wife," he said as he kissed her on the forehead. "But please promise to tell me as soon as it gets too much for you."

"I will," she promised, and gave him a warm kiss. They lay there listening to the constant pounding of the big rain drops, which fell from the trees onto the roof of the tent.

The rain stopped late that night. They resumed their journey in the morning amidst the fragrant smell of the wet grass. Both of them felt rested and good. The following three days were windy, and the sun hardly came out at all. Their wet clothes never had an opportunity to dry out.

The next town that they reached was Tibun. It was a small, forgotten place. The whole town consisted of thirty wooden shacks, which looked as if they were built about a thousand years ago. But the people were friendly and hospitable. They shared what little food they had with the travellers. When Natasha and Alexander left, they were full of food, news, and appreciation for the kindness of other human beings.

After a few more days of travelling, they reached the nearest train station. The stationmaster told them that they would have to wait two more days for the train to Moscow. Because it was summer the train was on time; and within three weeks, they arrived in the capital. Another long train ride took them north to Leningrad.

Leningrad was a harbor city and, consequently, was filled with people of all nationalities. There was also a large black market, which supplied foreign goods which the Soviet regime could not produce. It was a center of intrigue, and a booming business was done in the printing of false identity papers.

Alexander and Natasha had very little money and so were

able to afford only a cheap room. They found one on the waterfront. Alexander told Natasha to stay in the room while he went out to arrange passage.

"Don't be too long. I hate to be alone in this dark, awful room," she said.

Alexander searched all morning and most of the afternoon without being able to find someone who would agree to smuggle them out of Russia. He walked along the waterfront and asked every sailor he saw, but nobody was willing to help. Alexander did not want to leave Natasha alone any longer; but, at the same time, he did not want to return to her with bad news.

As Alexander was walking by a waterfront tavern, he heard a man playing the guitar and singing. The voice sounded oddly familiar. On an impulse, Alexander went in. What he saw startled him. The man playing the guitar was the same blond-haired youth who had been on the train with them when they went to Siberia. It was the same man who had stolen Natasha's warm coat.

The man recognized Alexander, also, and stopped playing. He sat in his chair and held the guitar in front of him, as if to protect himself from Alexander's wrath.

"How did you get here?" Alexander finally said.

"I had an uncle that I wanted to find, but it seems that he died years ago. Now I am just stuck here," the man said.

"And where is the young girl that you were with on the train?" Alexander asked.

"She left me a long time ago," the young man said.

"That's too bad," said Alexander.

"Everything happens for the best," the young man said philosophically. "But what brings you here?"

Alexander then proceeded to explain the situation to him. After Alexander finished, the young man sat for a few seconds without saying anything. Then he yelled for a waiter to bring two beers. It was while they were drinking the beers, that the young man told Alexander that he had a friend who, for a price, would probably be willing to smuggle Alexander and Natasha out of Russia.

Alexander ran back to Natasha to tell her the good news.

166

And the bad news. They would have to sell all their belongings, including the pearls that Grisha had given to Natasha.

That night, they sold everything, including the pearls; and, by the next morning, they found themselves on a fishing boat headed for Finland.

They did not come up onto the deck, until the Russian shoreline was miles away. They watched as it gradually faded behind the horizon. Tears filled their eyes, because they knew that they would probably never see their homeland again.

They were leaving behind them a land torn by turmoil, and a people they no longer understood. But they were also leaving behind another Russia, a Russia filled with hope and laughter, tall church steeples and gentle birch trees, and the feverish sound of the Balalaika.

They were leaving Russia now; but, at the same time, they were taking the best of Russia with them, the best of the old Russia. No matter where they lived, they would still be Russians, because their souls were Russian. For the best of Russia is not a place, but a spirit, a spirit that would live on in the hearts of their children long after the two of them had passed from this earth.

Alexander reached out and took Natasha's trembling body into his large bearlike arms. She pressed her head against his chest, and his strength flowed into her. As she pressed up against his shirt pocket, she could feel the good luck icon that she had given him.

The last vestige of land had disappeared some time ago. Alexander held Natasha's face between his gentle hands and kissed away each tear before it had a chance to run down her cheek. She knew that she loved him now. And she knew that she was ready to tell him so.

Her body was warmed by his embrace. All the aches and pains of the past were gone. Natasha knew that as long as she had Alexander by her side, she would have nothing to fear. Yes, she was ready for whatever destiny had in store for her.

POSTSCRIPT

Natasha died in childbirth just three days after we arrived in Switzerland. The baby lived for a few hours, and then died also. It was a girl. The past is ended now, and the time has come to extinguish all time. I have just drunk half the bottle of vodka that stands in front of me. The final moment has come. There is no more pain. Only emptiness. With my left hand, I pick up the revolver that lies on the desk; while with my right hand, I hold the pen which records these final instants. At once, I am actor and spectator. I cock the revolver with my thumb. It holds six bullets. I will need only one of them, I hope. I bring the barrel up to my left temple. I feel the cold steel against my warm flesh. The pressure allows me to feel my pulse. My eyes catch a final glimpse of the icon which Nata— —

My father, or more accurately, my stepfather died several days ago. He died of cancer approximately twenty-five years after he wrote the above manuscript. I found the manuscript in the safety deposit box in which he kept his will. In the same box, I also found the good luck icon that Grisha, my real father gave to my mother, and which she, in turn, gave to Alexander.

The icon is in my breast pocket now. I keep it with me at all times. One day, when I get married, I plan to give it to my wife.

It should be obvious to the reader that Alexander never did pull the trigger on that fateful day. This is the reason why.

It seems that my own little six-year-old self knocked on his door, just as he was about to. When he heard the knocking, he put the gun down and opened the door. When he saw me, I think he recognized that a part of his beloved Natasha was still alive, and as long as even a part of her was alive, he too still had a reason to go on living.

When grandmother died shortly after that of old age, I

moved in with Alexander; and he raised me. Together, we moved to a small town in the south of France. Alexander was the first real medical doctor that the town had; and as long as he was alive, he was the only one.

In a year or so, I, Fedya Grillow, will finish medical school. Then I will move back to that small town in the south of France and take over Alexander's practice, and, at the same time, try to keep alive the great love of humanity that was so dear to Alexander, Natasha, and every true Russian soul.

DATE DUE

DEMCO 38-297